"Joanna, I adore you."

"Casey, I don't believe you're doing this."

"Marry me."

"Not on your life."

The look of pretended ardor left his eyes; now they sparkled with challenge. "Is that a dare?"

Joanna decided the wiser course would be not to answer that particular question. "I'm not cut out to be a wife. The subject is closed." She held out her hand to him. "Come on. You make me nervous when you're on your knees."

"You know it's always a point of honor with me to beat you in a dare."

"One of these days, you're going to have to grow up," she said, not looking at him.

"I *am* grown up, Joey. The question is, are you?"

Joanna glanced up sharply at him. His gaze was probing, intense. She felt, for a moment, that there *was* a man inside him she hadn't yet met....

Dear Reader,

Welcome to the Silhouette **Special Edition** experience! With your search for consistently satisfying reading in mind, every month the authors and editors of Silhouette **Special Edition** aim to offer you a stimulating blend of deep emotions and high romance.

The name Silhouette **Special Edition** and the distinctive arch on the cover represent a commitment—a commitment to bring you six sensitive, substantial novels each month. In the pages of a Silhouette **Special Edition**, compelling true-to-life characters face riveting emotional issues—and come out winners. All the authors in the series strive for depth, vividness and warmth in writing these stories of living and loving in today's world.

The result, we hope, is romance you can believe in. Deeply emotional, richly romantic, infinitely rewarding—that's the Silhouette **Special Edition** experience. Come share it with us—six times a month!

From all the authors and editors of Silhouette **Special Edition**,

Best wishes.

CHRISTINE RIMMER

Double Dare

Published by Silhouette Books New York

America's Publisher of Contemporary Romance

For my parents, Auralee and Tom Smith,
who had love enough to give me my start in life—twice

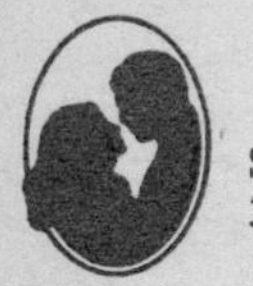

SILHOUETTE BOOKS
300 East 42nd St., New York, N.Y. 10017

DOUBLE DARE

ISBN: 0-373-09646-1

First Silhouette Books printing January 1991

Printed in the U.S.A.

Books by Christine Rimmer

Silhouette Desire

No Turning Back #418
Call it Fate #458
Temporary Temptress #602

Silhouette Special Edition

Double Dare #646

CHRISTINE RIMMER's

favorite pastimes include playing double-deck pinochle, driving long distances late at night, swimming in cold mountain rivers and eating anything with chocolate in it. She's also a voracious reader and an inveterate romantic daydreamer who's thrilled to have at last found a job that suits her perfectly: writing about the magical and exciting things that happen when two people fall in love. Christine lives in California with her young son, Jesse.

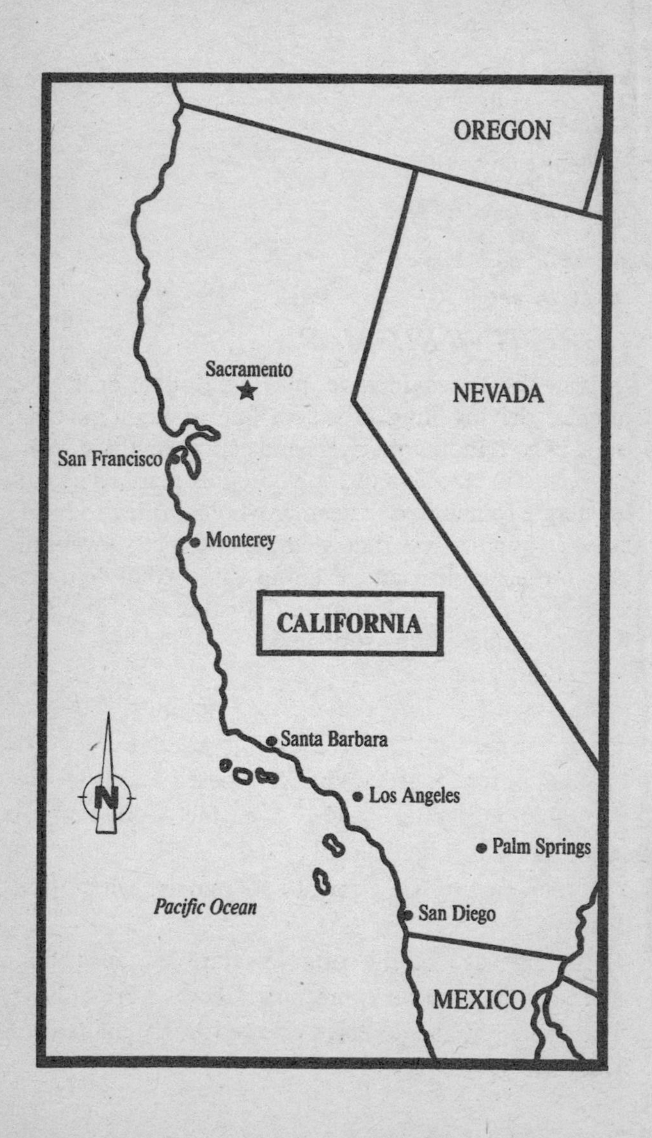
OREGON
NEVADA
Sacramento
San Francisco
Monterey
CALIFORNIA
Santa Barbara
N
Los Angeles
Palm Springs
Pacific Ocean
San Diego
MEXICO

Chapter One

"Joey?" the little boy asked.

Joanna paused in the act of turning off the light by the bed. "It's time to go to sleep, Mike," she said.

"I know, but Joey—"

She switched off the light. "No buts. Snuggle down." She tugged the sheet up around him. He smelled of toothpaste. When she kissed his cheek she thought that his skin was like some incredibly fine yet resilient flower. "'Night."

"Joey, just so you know. I won't go live with Uncle Burnett."

Joanna was glad the room was dark. Because of it, Mike couldn't see her expression. He was a bright boy. She probably should have guessed he might realize what was going on.

"Don't worry. It'll all work out for the best." The words were inane, but she heard herself saying them anyway as she stroked the fine hair back from his forehead.

"Uncle Burnett's always working. And Aunt Amanda's always smiling and asking me to be careful around her things." His tone turned plaintive. "I try to be careful, Joey. But jeez, I'm only almost six." He surged up from under the blanket and grabbed her in a ferocious hug.

"I want to be with you and Uncle Case," he whispered fiercely in her ear. "You could stay with us forever, if you wanted. You could paint your pictures here, Joey, just as good as down there by Disneyland. Say you will. Please, say yes."

Joanna hugged him back, saying nothing. Tears of love burned her eyes, and she willed them not to spill over and upset Mike even more. She wanted to say yes, to promise him all he desired. But making him a wild, unconsidered promise would be worse for him than for most five-year-olds. When he was still a baby he'd lost his father and his mother had died just five weeks ago. He deserved, as much as possible, only the kind of promises that could be kept.

Gently, she took his arms from around her neck and guided him back beneath the sheet. His narrow face was softly defined against the pillow. He watched her trustingly, full of conviction that a single word from her could guarantee his happiness.

Though she couldn't just say yes, neither could she deny him. "I'll do everything I can to see that you stay with your Uncle Case," she said.

His mouth, as small and neat as his mother's had been, curved upward. He uttered his favorite word: "Excellent." Then he said, "Now I can go to sleep." He rolled over on his side and tucked his fist beneath his chin.

Joanna watched his lashes come to rest on his cheeks. Then tiptoed out the door.

Before joining the family conference in the living room, Joanna paused in the hall bathroom. As she dabbed at her smudged mascara and ran a comb through her hair, she sent a little prayer to heaven that tonight would see an end to the conflict over who would have custody of Mike.

Actually, Joanna was feeling responsible. After Emily's funeral, Joanna hadn't returned to Southern California, where she'd lived for fourteen years. Instead, she'd stayed on in Sacramento to help out with Mike—and found herself getting increasingly involved in the dispute over Mike's future.

Tonight had been her idea. She'd talked Casey into fixing his famous Chicken Teriyaki, and she'd made the dessert crepes herself. She'd casually mentioned a "friendly talk" when she'd extended the invitation to Casey's older brother, Burnett, and his wife, Amanda. Joanna's plan had been to approach the disagreement in a civilized fashion, to create a relaxed, noncombative atmosphere in which to discuss the problem.

"Relaxed. Noncombative," she muttered to herself as she walked down the hall to the living room. She saw Burnett first. He stood beside the bar, clutching his wineglass a little too tightly. His stern face was slightly flushed.

Judging by Burnett's expression, things weren't going well. Joanna swallowed the knot in her throat and shifted her glance to Casey. He sat slouched in his favorite soft leather chair, one leg tossed over a chair arm and the other planted on the floor.

The differences between the brothers had always fascinated Joanna, making her wonder how two men could come from the same set of parents and yet be so diametrically opposite. There *were* family similarities: both had brown hair—though Burnett's was much darker—and the strong Clinton nose. But Casey had light, arresting eyes, while Burnett's were shadowy dark. Burnett stood a commanding six foot three and possessed an imposing physique. Casey was shorter, and cut from much finer stuff. He was Michelangelo's *David*, while Burnett could have been a latter-day Goliath.

In Joanna's memory, there had never been a subject on which Casey and Burnett had agreed. The clash over Mike was just another case in point—with one important difference. This time, a young child's future was at stake.

Forcing a composed smile, Joanna left the shadow of the hallway and moved to Casey's side. No one spoke. The short distance across the floor seemed like a hundred miles.

At the light touch of her hand on his shoulder, Casey glanced up. To a casual observer, he would have appeared utterly relaxed. But Joanna was not a casual observer. Casey Clinton had been her best friend for twenty-two years, ever since the day his mother, Lillian, had moved her family in next door to Joanna and her parents. Now, as Joanna looked down at him, the watchful silence lurking in his eyes struck her immediately, as did the barely perceptible tightness around his mouth.

"Did Mike give you any trouble?" he asked. Joanna knew the question was rhetorical. His mind was on the contest of wills between himself and his brother.

Joanna grinned at her friend, willing away the tension that filled the room. "He's like any five-year-old. He takes half an hour to brush his teeth. And then, of course, comes the story. And that final trip to the bathroom. But he did settle down finally."

The hostile silence descended again. Joanna glanced at Amanda, Burnett's wife. The porcelain-skinned blonde hovered near the French doors that led to the backyard. She stared out into the summer night as if there were something fascinating happening out by the pool.

Burnett drained his wineglass with an air of grim finality.

"More?" Joanna asked him politely, when he set his empty glass on the washed oak bar.

Burnett shook his head.

"I think I'd like another glass," Amanda chirped, her voice made shrill by her effort at nonchalance. "You just stay put. I spotted that bottle in the fridge." She laughed nervously. "I'll get it." Her heels clicked sharply on the pine-strip floor as she escaped to the kitchen. Joanna decided not to remind her that there was also a bottle in the bar icebox, right next to the feet of the glowering Burnett.

She couldn't blame Amanda for trying to find any excuse to leave the room. The Clinton brothers were going head-to-head, and that meant a possible explosion if Burnett lost his cool.

The silence after the sound of Amanda's clicking heels faded away reminded Joanna of a huge rubber band, stretching, stretching. To the snapping point.

Then Burnett broke the silence. "I only want what's best for my nephew." His deep voice vibrated with barely restrained animosity. "And I'm not going to let you prevent me from doing the right thing, no matter what foolish decisions Emily might have made."

"She was Mike's mother—" Casey began.

"She was confused," Burnett cut in with a haughty wave of his hand. "She never got over Michael's death. And she was always unrealistically indulgent toward you. I'll be frank. She looked up to you with stars in her eyes—her dashing brother, Casey, who dreamed of *flight*—" Burnett uttered the word as if it were an obscenity "—who deserted the family at eighteen to join the navy, and then came back to spend half his inheritance on a run-down airfield."

Burnett paused significantly. Joanna understood his ploy. He was hoping to put Casey on the defensive by getting him to defend Clinton Airfield. But Casey didn't bite. There was no reason to. The facts spoke for themselves. He had left the navy because his eyesight had deteriorated just enough for him to be grounded from flying the fighter jets he loved. He'd come home and bought the airfield. True, it would never make Casey much money—but Casey ran Clinton Airfield because flying was what he knew and loved. He had done what he wanted with his life, and done well at it.

"You were Emily's favorite," Burnett went on, when Casey didn't defend his choice of career. "That's all I'm saying. And she found me, well, mundane, to say the least. So, in choosing to make you Mike's legal guardian, she made an irresponsible decision. Besides, once she made up her mind, she was always as obstinate as you are." Burnett paused, then added with a sneer, "Whether she was right or not."

"I have no trouble supporting Mike," Casey said, remaining coolly reasonable. "I'm willing to spend time with him. And I love him. I wouldn't say that Emily made such a bad choice."

"Casey, you're a bachelor," Burnett replied. He flicked a dismissive glance around the spacious, comfortable, but very masculine room. "Your life lacks the necessary feminine touch." He shot Joanna a disparaging glance. "Except for Joanna's *generous* help, which we all know is only temporary at best."

"I'll be here to help out as long as Casey needs me," Joanna insisted in a level voice.

"Oh, come now, Joanna." Burnett eyed her with aloof disdain. "You're hardly cut out for domesticity. You'll be running back to L.A. to bury yourself in your canvasses and paintbrushes the first chance you get. You're simply not the type of woman who can be counted upon to take care of a child."

Beneath her hand, Joanna felt the slow tightening of Casey's muscles. She squeezed his shoulder gently, communicating in the subtle touch that she could handle his brother's calculated insults. She kept her face carefully composed, though the thread of bitterness in Burnett's tone had distressed her.

I should have realized, she thought. He's never completely forgiven me.

Fourteen years ago, Joanna had come dangerously close to marrying Burnett. Casey had changed her mind for her. And he'd done it in a very unconventional way. Burnett himself had actually broken things off, and over the years Joanna had allowed herself to believe that bygones were bygones. But as she faced Burnett now over another issue altogether, she saw she was mistaken. Burnett still thought that she'd made a fool of him, and deep down he still nurtured resentment toward her.

Joanna realized it had been foolish for her to have arranged this family dinner. She should have stayed out of it, and let Burnett and Casey fight it out in their own way. But now it was too late.

"I'll say it again, Burnett." Joanna's voice remained steady and firm. "I'll be here to help out as long as Casey needs me."

Burnett's lips curled contemptuously. "How convenient for him."

Out of the corner of her eye, she spied Casey's dangling foot. It was clad in a high-top sneaker and it had begun beating rhythmically in the air. Joanna swallowed. If she didn't put Burnett firmly in his place on this issue, Casey would do it for her. And the Lord only knew how he would manage that.

That was the thing about Casey. He could be pushed so far and never even raise his voice. He'd be smiling. And reasonable, and even rather good-natured. And then *it* would happen. He'd toss a curve that the most experienced verbal batter could never hit. As his friend, Joanna would be the one wearing the catcher's glove.

Straightening her shoulders, Joanna said, "It's not a matter of Casey's convenience. It goes far beyond that. I'm Casey's friend, and I'll always be there for him if he needs me. Furthermore, Emily herself asked me to help out."

"When exactly did she do that?" Burnett demanded.

Casey cut in. "Burnett," he said, "she doesn't owe you any explanations."

"It's okay." Joanna smiled down into Casey's eyes, willing him not to say or do anything he'd regret later. Then she looked back at Burnett. "It was a couple of years ago. Emily brought Mike down to visit Disneyland. They stayed in West Hollywood with me. We talked." Joanna paused, remembering Emily's pixieish face as she sat across from her at her own kitchen table, seeing again the melancholy in Emily's eyes...

"It took me a year to believe that Michael was really dead," Emily had confided, her sad eyes focused on some faraway place. Mike, Sr. had been killed in a freak motorcycle accident a few years before that. Those who knew how much Emily loved her husband had feared for a while that Emily would never recover from the loss.

"In some ways, I still don't believe he's gone," Emily had said. "I still look up from something I'm doing and expect to see him there, sitting across from me, or standing in the doorway. And when I'm finally aware that he's not really there, there's this horrible moment, this emptiness, when I realize he's never going to be there again..." Emily's voice had trailed off then; she'd forced a smile. "Sorry. You asked," she'd said a moment later, with an embarrassed little clearing of her throat. "Sometimes I wish I had what you have with your painting, Joey. Something to lose myself in, you know?"

Joanna had nodded. For a time they'd fallen into a companionable silence, and Joanna, with her artist's habit of observation, had recorded the moment in her mind. Two women, one dark-haired and one light, sitting at a kitchen table bathed in a hard wedge of blinding morning sun.

"I've always thought of you as a sister, did you know that?" Emily had said at last.

And then she'd begun to talk about the will she'd made...

"You talked about what?" Burnett prompted, yanking Joanna's thoughts back to the present.

Joanna sighed, letting her precious memories of Emily fade into the past. Then slowly and carefully she began to explain what Emily had told her.

"Emily said she wanted her wishes clearly understood, in case anything happened to her. She said she wanted Casey to raise Mike. She said she'd asked Casey and he had agreed. She also said that she'd explained her feelings to your mother and that Lillian understood completely."

"You don't have to tell me why she didn't choose Mother," Burnett cut in gruffly. "Mother deserves a few years of freedom. What I want to know is, why did she decide against me?" Burnett could not entirely mask the thread of anguish beneath his stiffly spoken words. For a man who exerted such rigid control over every aspect of his life, accepting the death of a loved one was no mean feat. Joanna felt compassion for him rise up within her. Burnett could be a hard man, but he still had feelings. She really didn't want to tell him why Emily had chosen Casey over him. The reason would hurt him.

"Joanna," Burnett said, prodding her. "I asked you a direct question."

Once again Joanna looked rather hopelessly at Casey. His eyes said, There's no getting around it now. You'll have to tell him.

Joanna dragged in a breath and faced Burnett squarely. "She felt you had a problem with showing love. She said she could never leave Mike to be raised without love."

An awful silence ensued. Then Burnett said, too quietly. "Of course I don't believe that. I—" he paused over the word, as if it were in bad taste to say it in mixed company "—*love* Mike. And I know what he needs." He paused to look for his wife. "Amanda?" She appeared on cue, as if, after having left the kitchen, she'd been lurking behind the big areca palm in the foyer. She glided to Burnett's side, and he put his arm around her.

"Amanda and I," Burnett continued, "have talked this over." They smiled at each other, automatically and without any discernable warmth. Joanna thought they looked like a commercial for the perfect couple. He, handsome and dark. She, lovely and blond. "And we know we're in the right."

Casey said, "It doesn't matter what you know, Burnett. Mike's staying with me." His foot kept tapping. Relentlessly.

Burnett turned his cold smile on his brother. "No, Casey. He is not staying with you."

Joanna had a horrible, sinking feeling in her stomach. Burnett had moved right past blustery rage, which was awful but could be handled, to cold-blooded calculation. And Casey's foot kept tapping faster and faster.

Burnett threw out his challenge.

"We've taken it to a lawyer, Casey," Burnett said.

Casey moved his shoulder just enough to shake off Joanna's restraining hand. "You're planning to *sue* me for custody? You'll drag Mike through the courts just to prove Emily wrong for choosing me over you?" In spite of the anger implicit in his words, he asked the question very calmly.

"I want to raise the boy because it's the right thing for him," Burnett said crisply. "And I'll win, too. You know I will. My lawyers agree with me. A two-parent home will be best for Mike."

"I see," said Casey. "That's your case, then? That I'm single, and you're not."

"You can't win in this, Casey."

For a moment, Casey stared at his brother.

And then, very slowly, he smiled. "Don't bet on it, Big Brother."

Joanna's stomach tightened with dread. Something completely impossible would be coming out of Casey's mouth next, Joanna knew it with every fiber of her being.

Casey went on. "You'd better see your lawyers again, then. And this time be sure to give them our news."

"What news?" Burnett asked suspiciously.

Casey snared Joanna's hand. His touch was warm against Joanna's skin which now felt cold with dread.

Casey squeezed her hand. He shot her a look that managed to be both fond and crackling with challenge. How well she knew that look. A dare. They had dared each other often over the years. And what did the dares usually get them? Trouble.

Joanna gave Casey's hand a returning squeeze. A desperate squeeze. A squeeze that said *this is no time for dares....*

But Casey Clinton ignored her unspoken plea.

He said, "Joey and I have decided to get married."

Chapter Two

Amanda gave a strangled little squeak that sounded like the cry of a trapped mouse. After that, you could have heard a pin drop in Fresno, two hundred miles away.

Joanna could have killed Casey right then. She *would* have killed him if it wasn't absolutely imperative that they present a united front.

"You're lying," said Burnett at last.

Casey said nothing. Maintaining a murderous grip on her best friend's hand, Joanna spoke the words she'd never in a million years expected to utter. "It's true, Burnett. Casey and I are getting married right away."

Burnett glared at Joanna for suspended seconds, as if the force of his will could make her retract her words. When she didn't recant, he pounded a fist on the bar and bellowed, "This is outrageous!"

Looking stunned, Amanda clutched her husband's arm. "Can they do that, darling?" she asked in a bewildered little-girl voice.

Burnett ignored her. His eyes were on Joanna. "You're lying, aren't you? Both of you. Just admit the truth now."

Joanna almost did just that. But then she thought of how that would make Casey look, how Burnett would hold it up as more evidence that Casey was too irresponsible to raise a child.

"We're getting married," Joanna repeated, and waited for Casey to say the same.

But he was silent. Joanna eased her death grip on his hand and wondered if he was already trying to formulate a way out of the mess he'd gotten them into. It was, strangely, as if they were kids again and Casey had set off the fire alarm down on the corner just to see what it would sound like. He'd been caught, of course, and punished. But not before Joanna had tried to protect him by claiming she was the culprit.

Burnett turned on Casey again. "You're just stirring up trouble. Because you can't win in this, you want to create as much static as you can before you finally give in."

"Mike's staying with me," Casey said quietly. "And now—it's been a hell of an evening, and I'm tired." He swung his dangling foot to the ground and stood up, letting go of Joanna's hand in the process.

Though she was furious with him, his touch had been reassuring. For a moment, standing there alone, Joanna felt cast adrift. But then she reminded herself that they were still in this dilemma together. And together they could find a way out.

They needed to talk, that was all. But first, they must get rid of Burnett and Amanda.

Joanna trotted briskly to the dining alcove where Amanda had left her handbag. Then she hustled back to the living room. She handed Amanda the purse.

"Thanks for coming." She smiled at Amanda, and then turned a level stare on the scowling Burnett. "I'm sorry it couldn't have been a more... mutually satisfying evening."

Casey came and stood behind Burnett. Between the two of them, he and Joanna managed to herd the other couple toward the door.

"This isn't the end of it," Burnett warned. "This incredible announcement of yours only makes me more determined to see that that child gets a proper home."

"Good night, Big Brother," said Casey, hanging back a little and feigning a jaunty wave.

Burnett was still growling when Joanna closed the door.

Feeling suddenly deflated, Joanna leaned against the door. She reached down to slip off her high-heeled sandals, which she let drop by the areca palm in the corner nearby.

Suddenly the brightly lit, roomy house seemed very quiet. Joanna stared down at her toes for a minute, curling and uncurling them against the cool stone vestibule floor. Then she looked up at Casey.

He stood near the entrance to the living room, his hands in the pockets of his loose tan slacks. He wore an inscrutable expression. He seemed to be studying her.

She had no idea why she felt so defensive.

"What?" she asked, in that cryptic verbal shorthand that they often used with each other.

"What do you mean, what?"

"What are you staring at?" Her question came out sounding as defensive as she was feeling.

"You." His mouth wore a hint of a smile.

"Well, I know that. But why?"

"Why what?"

She knew that he knew what she'd meant, but she slowly explained anyway. "Why are you staring at me?"

"It's okay," he said, as if he were talking to himself.

"What's okay?"

"Staring at you," he said. "I like it, always have. That's important, don't you think? That you like staring at the person you're going to spend the rest of your life with."

Joanna groaned aloud. He *couldn't* be thinking of actually going through with it—could he? "Now, just a minute—" she began.

But he didn't let her finish. "Come on," he said, and covered the distance between them.

"Where?" Wary of him after what he'd done, she shrank against the door, her hands behind her back. He reached out and felt for her wrist, pulling it out from behind her.

"Outside," he said. And then he towed her along behind him as he made for the French doors on the other side of the living room. "I'm sick of being cooped up in here."

He paused long enough to scoop up two glasses and get the bottle of wine from under the bar.

Beyond the French doors, it was a beautiful evening, mild for July in the Sacramento Valley, which was known for its hot summer days and oppressively warm nights.

"Much better," he said, when they stood by the night-lighted pool.

Since Casey's house was in a development outside of Sacramento, the lights of the central valley sprawl could be seen as a glow on the horizon. A half-moon beamed down on them. And the stars, though paled by the city lights, still looked close enough to touch.

"Too bad about the moon," Casey mused, much too lightheartedly for Joanna's peace of mind. "I swear, Joey. If I'd known what was going to happen tonight, I would have put in an order for a big, fat full moon."

Joanna gave a low growl of frustration, freed her wrist, hiked up her skirt and sat down at the edge of the pool, dangling her feet in the water and not looking at him. Casey sat beside her, but back from the edge. She heard him pull the cork from the bottle and pour out the chilled wine.

Then she felt the cold kiss of a glass on her arm as he touched her with it by way of offering it to her. Instinctively, she jerked away.

Casey chuckled. "Whew. You *are* steamed, aren't you?"

She turned her head enough so she could glare at him. "What do you expect?" Grudgingly, she took her wine from him.

He raised his glass to her. "Tears of joy that I'm willing to make an honest woman of you after all these years?"

"An honest woman? You make an honest woman out of a mistress or a lover. Not out of your very best friend whom you've never done more than kiss."

"I was thinking more on the lines of emotionally honest," he told her, still in that infuriatingly nonchalant tone.

"What are you saying? We're friends. That's emotionally honest."

"Joey, you certainly are defensive about this."

Joanna gaped at him. This conversation was not going at all the way she'd meant it to. Not that she'd had time to decide exactly how it should go. She hadn't even had time to so much as draw in a calming breath since he'd announced to Burnett that they were headed for the altar.

"Defensive is not the issue," she snapped.

"Oh, no. Then what is?"

"How we're going to get out of it."

He leaned back on an elbow. He was still grinning. "Maybe I don't want to get out of it. Maybe it's time I settled down and learned to live with emotional commitment."

"Fine. You do that. Just leave me out of it."

"I'm sorry, Joey." He didn't look at all contrite. "But I can't leave you out of it. You're too perfect."

"You're nuts." She glared at him, and then looked away into the lights at the bottom of the pool. "I'm not cut out for domesticity. Burnett was right about that much, at least."

"That doesn't matter." Joanna turned once again to stare disbelievingly at him. "Cooking and cleaning always get done one way or another," he said. "What I'm talking about is how perfect you and I really are for each other."

He set his glass aside, drew up his knees and wrapped his arms around them. "I don't know why I didn't see it before. The obvious solution to the problem is for us to get married. I mean, we're both committed to Mike. And to each other in all the ways that count. You're always there for me, and vice versa. We have a history together, things in common that go back years and years. We practically read each other's minds—"

She cut him off. "But we're not in love with each other." She looked away toward the lava rock fountain that bubbled into the pool on the other side.

For a moment, he was silent. She thought she'd finally given him pause. But then he said, "It's a stupid idea anyway, that people should marry because they're in love. Why base a lifetime commitment on two sets of crazed hormones?"

"I'd prefer to be in love, thank you."

He seemed to have no reply for that. She continued to stare at the fountain. Then she heard his teasing voice again.

"Joey..." He reached out and smoothed her hair from underneath, the pad of his index finger whispering along her neck. It was the kind of thing he did all the time, a fond gesture of caring, of closeness.

But, suddenly, for the first time in years, it seemed charged with new meaning.

"Don't—" She ducked away.

He withdrew his hand. "Come on. It's not such a bad idea."

"It's impossible," she said, still refusing to look at him.

There was a long silence. Over by the fountain, a cricket chirped.

Joanna felt trapped. When Casey had made the announcement, she hadn't even considered that he would actually want to go through with it. Now, she not only had to think of a way to ease out of the bind with Burnett, but she also had to convince her friend that a marriage between the two of them was totally out of the question.

Casey chuckled.

"What?" she said, automatically turning around to look at him again, wanting, as always, to share in the joke.

"Just thinking."

"Thinking what?"

"If you painted us now, what you'd call it."

Joanna knew she shouldn't ask what. "What?"

"The Marriage Proposal?"

She tried gentle reason. "It's really not a good idea, Casey. You have to accept that, then we can start thinking about how we're going to handle Burnett."

His gray-blue eyes still held a hint of teasing humor. "Why is it such a bad idea? Have you been holding out on me? Is there a new man in your life?" He gave her his gorgeous fly-boy smile.

She refused to smile back, though maintaining a serious expression took some effort. Casey had always had a devastating smile. Too often, he could get her to do anything he wanted just by smiling like that. "No," she said. "There's no one."

"Not for me, either. See? We're just getting to be a couple of confirmed bachelors. Marriage. To each other. It's the only answer."

Joanna groaned. "Why are you being so stubborn about this?"

He stopped smiling and said nothing for a moment. The cricket kept up its cheerful song. "I have Mike to think about," he finally said.

Their eyes locked. He *would* have to bring the focus around to Mike.

She thought of Burnett, willing to throw them all into a lengthy court battle to get his way. And she thought of Mike, who could end up the *almost*-six-year-old victim of a lifelong war for dominance between two brothers. If Casey were married, Burnett would have no case at all—as long as the marriage provided a stable environment in which to raise a child.

If they decided to go through with it they would have to convince everyone that they were marrying because they wanted to bind their lives together in the truest sense of the word. Mike would only be benefiting from a decision that Casey and Joanna would have made anyway.

It wouldn't be so difficult to make the world believe they were in love, Joanna mused. No one else really understood the nature of their friendship anyway. Burnett, she was sure, actually believed that she and Casey had been lovers for years. Why not just let everyone think that they'd finally decided to make it legal?

The upstairs room she was staying in would be fine for a permanent studio. She could make Sacramento her base, rather than her West Hollywood apartment. And getting back and forth to Los Angeles to maintain her professional contacts there would present no problem. After all, Casey did own an airfield.

"You know it would work," Casey said softly, as if he could tell from her expression exactly what was going on in her mind.

"No, I don't," she lied, angry at her own mind for wandering off into dangerous conjecture about something she had no intention of doing.

"Yes, you do."

"I don't."

"Do."

"Don't."

"Do..."

They both sounded the way they had when they were children. Against her will, Joanna felt a smile coming on. "Will you stop it?" she begged.

"Then marry me." He grabbed her hand and started towing her to her feet.

"Casey..." she pleaded, trying to object.

But he was already taking her wine, setting it aside and pulling her toward the umbrella-shaded glass-topped picnic table on the edge of the lawn.

"Sit here," he said, and pushed her down into a padded lawn chair.

"Casey, no—"

He knelt before her. "Joanna, my darling—"

"Get up, you rat."

"Marry me and I'll give you two sunsets in one day, one on the ground and—"

"One in the air. I've heard it before." And she had, too. Years ago, in high school, he'd asked her what romantic words to say to a girl. She'd told him. In detail. And now she heard the flowery adolescent phrases she'd invented for him coming right back at her.

"I'll give you the sky—" he went on.

"Right. And the top of the clouds—"

"We'll touch the stars—"

"I know, I know. And swing from the moon."

"Joanna, I adore you. Let me take you to heaven on the wings of the night."

"I don't believe you're doing this."

He put his hand over the little alligator embroidered on his shirt. "I can't live without you."

"Fine. You won't have to. Lately, I'm here all the time anyway."

"Marry me."

"Not on your life."

The look of feigned ardor left his eyes; instead, they sparked with challenge. "I dare you to marry me."

Joanna decided the wiser course would be to pretend he hadn't said that. She said, "I'm not cut out to be a wife. The subject is closed." She held out her hand to him. "Come on. Stand up. You make me nervous when you're on your knees."

He took her hand and stood. "The dare's been made, Joey. Accept it."

She straightened the full peasant skirt of her dress over her crossed knees. "One of these days, you're going to have to grow up," she said, not looking at him.

"I *am* grown-up, Joey. The question is, are you?"

Joanna glanced up sharply at him. His gaze was probing, intense. She felt, for a moment, that inside him was a man who was a stranger to her.

But then he smiled, and he was just Casey again. He shrugged and left to retrieve their glasses and the bottle of wine over by the rim of the pool. Joanna watched him, her artist's mind intrigued by the lean economy of his movements, by the way the pool lights shot brightness upward over his face as he bent to get the glasses, bathing his features in an eerie, rippling glow.

He returned and set her glass beside her on the picnic table. "I'm turning in," he said.

"You can't," she protested. "We have to talk about how we're going to handle Burnett."

"We'll get married right away," he told her. "That'll handle the problem just fine." His tone was the same as the one he would have used to tell her he was headed for the corner store to get a loaf of bread and a carton of milk.

"Absolutely not," she said.

"Joey," he reached down and chucked her under the chin, "a dare's a dare. Say yes."

"I'm not going to marry you."

"Remember Graeagle, Joey," he said cryptically. "Once you swore you'd marry Burnett and I swore you wouldn't. Who was right then?"

"You were," she readily agreed. "You said marriage would keep me from doing what I was meant to do."

"I said marriage to *the wrong guy* would be a disaster."

"And all of a sudden, after all these years, you've decided *you're* the right guy?"

"Look. I know we can be happy together. And we can give Mike what he needs. Think about that."

"Casey—"

But he would hear no more. He bent and kissed her on the forehead.

And then he went back inside.

Joanna sat alone for a while. Then she checked on Mike in his ground floor bedroom, reclaimed her sandals from the vestibule and climbed the stairs.

At the top of the landing she hesitated, considering going on to Casey's room. But she decided she had no idea what she wanted to say to him right then. She shook her head and opened the first door at the top of the stairs.

Once alone in the room that she'd started to think of as "hers" over the past five weeks, Joanna stepped out of her dress and tossed it across the back of a chair. Leaving on her slip she dropped her sandals by her drawing board.

Right after Emily died and Joanna had decided to remain for an open-ended visit, Casey had insisted that she set up the room as a studio. Besides the drawing board and easel, there were materials for stretching canvasses as well as a long folding table covered with art supplies.

The big bay windows on two of the walls drew the sun into the room, so that in the daytime it was washed with light. Though the view was of landscaped yards and gracious homes rather than the tarred rooftops of West Hollywood, the space itself was not that much different from the living room in her apartment, which Joanna used as her studio space at home.

For a moment, in the darkness, Joanna spared a guilty thought for all the work she hadn't been doing lately. She considered throwing on a robe and then sketching for a while before she went to bed. But she gave up on the idea; her mind was simply too preoccupied with her best friend and his outrageous announcement.

We can be happy together, Casey's words replayed in her head. And we can give Mike what he needs... Remember Graeagle...

The crazy events in Graeagle, the tiny Sierra foothill town where the Clintons owned a vacation cabin, had happened fourteen years ago. It was the summer that they had graduated from high school, the summer after Joanna's father died. Looking back, Joanna realized that she'd started seeing Burnett because her mother had approved of him. Joanna had wanted, impossibly, to make it up to her mother for losing her father. She'd longed to ease her mother's pain by becoming the kind of daughter that her mother had always wanted her to be.

But Casey Clinton had had other plans. And his actions then had been every bit as outrageous as those of tonight.

In hindsight, Joanna knew that her friend's outrageousness had saved her from a life she had never been meant to live. She would always be grateful to him for that.

But, she told herself firmly, being grateful doesn't mean I should marry him now.

In the small, functional bathroom that shared a wall with Casey's large, sybaritic one, she brushed her teeth. Then she returned to her room and climbed beneath the covers of a daybed.

Sleep, however, didn't come. She kept thinking about Graeagle.

Late on a Saturday afternoon in July, Casey had come to the door of her mother's house with some absurd story about needing her help getting his Bronco started. Totally unsuspecting, Joanna had followed him next door to his mother's garage where he'd grabbed her from behind, trussed her up like a prize turkey and driven off with her wedged behind the seats so no one would see he was abducting her.

Joanna smiled into the darkness. It had been an uncomfortable ride, bouncing around back there, whining and pleading while Casey occasionally tossed a sympathetic remark over his shoulder at her.

I hate to do this, Joey, but you didn't leave me any damn choice... Someday, you'll thank me for this... You're my best friend, I can't let you ruin your life....

When the bouncing and rolling of the truck had finally stopped, Casey had dragged her out by the feet, slung her over his shoulder and carried her, bucking and squirming, into the cabin. There, he'd locked her in for an entire night and for half of the next day while he badgered her relentlessly to break it off with his brother. He urged her to go to UCLA as she'd planned.

But he hadn't been able to keep her locked up forever. In the early afternoon, she'd grabbed his keys and bolted out the door.

He'd caught up with her at the tin-roofed garage, but she'd eluded him. So he'd chased her out behind the house, bringing her down on a scratchy bed of pine needles beneath the tall trees. They'd struggled.

He'd gained the top position, his bluejeaned knees planted on either side of her hips. She'd kept trying to punch him. But then he'd captured her wrists, pinning them to the prickly bed of pine needles beneath them.

He'd begged her to listen to reason, but she had only fought harder, insisting she loved Burnett. He'd called her a liar, and then announced bluntly that he knew she'd never made love with his brother.

"Your body knows the truth," he'd told her. "It shies away from him. Your body knows my brother will never let you be your real self. You can say you're waiting for marriage and all that, and a lot of people might even believe you. But this is Casey you're talking to, Joey. I'd never buy a story like that from you. You're not the type to hold out for a ring on your finger. If the trust and love were there, you'd be all over a guy like paint."

Not wanting to hear the truth in his words, Joanna had begun struggling again, demanding he let her up.

"Not yet." A cunning gleam had lit in his eyes. "I'm going to prove I'm right first..."

And then he'd kissed her. The only *real* kiss they'd ever shared.

With that kiss, Casey had proved she was lying to herself. Had she truly been in love with Burnett, then Casey's kiss never could have stirred her the way it did.

Joanna punched her pillow and rearranged it under her head. The kiss, really, had meant nothing, she told herself. There was no need to give it too much thought. He'd kissed her and she'd liked it; Casey had only done it because he wanted her to reconsider her plan to marry Burnett.

It was what followed the kiss that was important. He'd asked her, for the sake of their friendship, to stay until dark. She'd agreed. And through the rest of that afternoon and evening she had come back in touch with who she really was and what she wanted to do with her life. Casey had provided her with a sketch pad and soft pencils, and insisted that she spend the time drawing.

By the time they returned to Sacramento, Joanna knew Casey was right, though she didn't know how she was going to break it off with Burnett.

She needn't have worried. As soon as Burnett heard that she'd stayed with Casey longer than she'd had to, he'd asked for his ring back.

Joanna had felt ten pounds lighter after she'd handed it to him.

She'd left to look for an apartment near UCLA two weeks later. She saw Casey just once before she left. He came over with the sketch pad she'd left in his Bronco. He was wearing dark glasses that didn't completely cover either the big shiner or the bruise on his left cheek.

''You should see Burnett,'' he'd offered wryly as he'd handed her the pad.

"No, thanks. Do you want to come in?"

"Uh-uh. Gotta go. See you..." And he'd left. He was headed for the navy, on his way toward fulfilling his dream of testing fighter jets. He hadn't promised to write, or to look her up between basic training and whatever came next for him. She'd understood. They were each starting a new life, and holding on to the old was too dangerous then.

She'd put the sketch pad away in her closet, because at that moment it would have made her sad to look at the drawings inside. When she moved to Los Angeles she forgot about the drawings. And when her mother took the insurance windfall from her father's death and moved into the big brick house in South Land Park, the sketch pad somehow was lost. But it was okay. There was so much to paint in the world, so many scenes and moments to capture. An afternoon and evening spent in Graeagle with her best friend wasn't something that clamored for her attention as time went by.

Now, though, as she lay awake in her studio in her best friend's house, she wondered what had happened to the sketch pad. She wondered if the sketches were as good as she had thought they were.

Probably not, she decided, so it was just as well that she'd never know. Let them remain perfect in her memory.

Joanna rolled over and faced the wall. She closed her eyes. In no time at all, she was dreaming.

"Joey?" The soft whisper came to her out of the darkness.

The dream she'd been having melted around her, and Joanna found herself sitting up in the daybed in Casey's house, clutching the blanket to her breasts. With her free hand, she rubbed the grogginess from her eyes and raked her hair back from her face.

"Casey?" She could see the outline of his torso, the beautiful, spare musculature of his shoulders, and the shadow of his head against the window. He was half sitting, with one leg resting on the window seat in the bay window opposite her bed. The only item of clothing he had on were the slacks he'd worn that night.

She squinted at him, trying to focus on him. It was dark, but he was outlined in moonlight. "What is it?"

She knew he was watching her, though she couldn't see his eyes. "I couldn't sleep," he said.

She clutched the covers a little closer against herself, feeling at a disadvantage, half-asleep and bathed in moonlight before the eyes she knew so well but in the darkness couldn't see.

He was behaving so uncharacteristically, entering her room without warning. If there was one thing they had both always respected, it was each other's privacy. But then, she reminded herself, everything between them had suddenly changed. He had dared her to marry him.

And never had she been able to refuse one of his dares.

"Thinking about us?" she asked.

"Yeah."

When he didn't go on, she tried to bridge the awkward silence by saying, "I was dreaming."

"About what?"

Joanna secured the sheet around herself and leaned back against the bolsters. She closed her eyes briefly, calling up the dream he'd interrupted.

"It was at the first Chilly Lilly's," she said, referring to the chain of ice cream stores that Casey's mother had started and Burnett now operated. "I was twelve again, and I was calling for you. When you came, you were an adult. I was all upset that you'd gone and grown up without me."

He turned his head, and she saw his profile, the strong Clinton nose making it resemble a profile on a Roman coin. "Sounds pretty scary to me," he said. He remained turned away from her, looking out the window at the shingled roof of the house next door.

"It wasn't scary. Not really,' she said.

"It was only a dream, anyway," he said when she didn't go on.

"Yes. Just a dream."

He stood up then. "I can't stop thinking about this," he said, and she knew he was referring to their possible marriage. "I want us to settle the matter." His voice, low and serious, lacked any trace of his usual humor.

Her throat felt thick. It was so eerie. Limned in moonlight, he could have been anyone. He could have been the dark prince of her most primal romantic fantasy. Her own private Heathcliff, her other half come to claim her.

"Tonight?" she asked, the question husky and hesitant.

"Yeah. I want you to say yes. I know it can work. We can make it work."

She thought about how much she owed him, and the promises she'd made to both his sister and to Mike.

"Say yes," he prompted.

He moved toward her, a shadow with substance crossing the smooth wood floor.

Her answer surprised her with its steadiness. "All right," she said. "I'll marry you, Casey."

He came no closer. He nodded. "Good night, then, Joey," he said, and was gone.

Chapter Three

"The garden looks lovely," Casey's mother, Lillian, said. Lillian was standing at the window, gazing down on the guests in the garden below.

Joanna stared at her own reflection in the vanity table mirror, finding it hard to believe that the bride who gazed back at her was really herself.

"How your mother managed to orchestrate all this in less than two weeks is beyond my comprehension," Lillian remarked.

Joanna brushed at the skirt of her magnolia-white crepe georgette dress, her thoughts turning to her own mother. Joanna had been surprised at how readily Marie Vail had sanctioned this marriage.

All through Joanna's childhood Marie's fondest wish had been that "that wild Casey Clinton" would drop off the face of the earth—and take Joanna's art supplies along with him.

But, over the years, when she'd seen how happy Joanna was with the life she'd chosen, Marie had changed her opinion. All she'd asked for, when Joanna told her that she and Casey were going to get married, was the privilege of giving her daughter a garden wedding in her own backyard.

Lillian turned from the window and smiled at Joanna, her hazel eyes lighting in appreciation. "You look beautiful."

Joanna made a face at herself in the mirror and then smoothed the low sweetheart neckline of her dress. "I feel kind of frazzled."

"Well, no one will guess. You look stunningly composed." Lillian left the window to come and stand behind her. Setting her clutch purse on a corner of the vanity table, Lillian bent over and brushed her cheek against Joanna's. The touch was feather-light, in consideration of Joanna's hair, which had been swept up in a soft Gibson girl style and threaded with tiny white silk flowers.

"My son's a lucky man," Lillian breathed in her ear.

Joanna immediately felt her frayed nerves relaxing. For Joanna, Lillian Clinton had always had the ability to put things in perspective. All it took was a reassuring touch from Casey's mother and the roughest challenge seemed easily surmountable.

She smiled at Lillian in the mirror.

"Is Casey even here?" she asked wryly. "I've spent so much time getting ready for today that we've hardly seen each other lately. If he's changed his mind about marrying me, I wouldn't even know."

Though Joanna didn't mention it, her work had also suffered. She hadn't picked up a brush or her sketch pad since the night Casey had told his brother about the marriage. And Lord knew she hadn't been doing all that much before that. Since Emily's funeral, her creative life seemed to have come to a standstill.

Joanna couldn't afford the hiatus, either. The small gallery in Los Angeles that exhibited her work had agreed to give her her own show in September. She'd promised Althea Gatin, the gallery owner, some new pieces. But she hadn't come up with even a ghost of an idea for anything new. In the past two months, her life had changed so drastically that she was beginning to wonder if things would ever seem normal again.

Lillian's hand rested comfortingly on her shoulder. Joanna gave it a companionable squeeze.

"I'm sure things will settle down after today," Joanna said, pushing her anxieties about her work to the back of her mind.

"And you don't need to worry," Lillian teased. "I saw Casey not five minutes ago. He looked fine. Not the least likely to leave you waiting at the altar." Lillian scooped up her clutch purse from the table and stepped back. "Now stand up and let's admire you."

Joanna obligingly pushed back the vanity stool and went to twirl before the mirrored wall of the closet. The calf-length dress floated around her deliciously, the crepe so light it was like a spun breeze. The long raglan sleeves draped softly in tiny gathers that were repeated at either side of the silk-buttoned bodice.

"Something old?" Lillian asked.

Joanna shot her a puzzled look before catching on. "I completely forgot."

Lillian pretended to look disapproving. "Well, the dress is new. How about borrowed?"

Joanna grinned smugly, and touched the pearl clip that nestled with the little flowers in her hair. "This is Mother's."

"And blue?"

Joanna lifted a froth of white crepe to reveal her powder-blue garter.

"Good, but you need something old," Lillian insisted. "It's a tradition."

"It doesn't matter. I've never been a very traditional woman anyway."

"Don't say that," Lillian chided, "or you'll ruin my surprise." Wearing a Mona Lisa smile, she slipped the catch on her clutch purse and extracted a midnight-blue satin bag.

"Maybe this will help." The satin bag was old, creased in places, but very fine. Lillian loosened the drawstring. "Hold out your hand."

Joanna obeyed and a five-strand pearl choker, bound with an enhancer of ice-bright diamonds, dropped into her palm. Joanna had seen the necklace once before, on the day that Emily had married Michael Nevis.

"It belonged to my grandmother," Lillian said. "She gave it to my mother on the day of her wedding, and my mother handed it down to me when I married. I was fortunate to see my own daughter wear it on her wedding day." Lillian's voice had become, suddenly, very low and controlled. "And then it came back to me . . . when Emily died."

Joanna looked up from the pearls as Lillian glanced away.

"Lillian?"

"Oh, this is awful. I wasn't going to cry."

Diffidently, Joanna touched Lillian's shoulder. The older woman stiffened, and then swayed toward Joanna, allowing Joanna to wrap comforting arms around her.

"I'll muss your beautiful hair,' Lillian sighed.

"So what?" Joanna held on.

"Oh, Joey. I miss her so."

"I know. We all do."

"And how she'd have loved to have been here today. You and Casey were two of her favorite people, you know."

Down in the yard, the pianist Marie had hired was playing a slow ballad that had been popular a decade before.

For a moment, Joanna wished fervently that she hadn't chosen the song. It was too sad for a wedding. But then, in her mind, she saw Emily . . .

As a skinny little girl in pink shorts with scabs on her knees, hanging upside down from a jungle gym bar: "Casey, Joey, watch me now!"

At thirteen, her strawberry-blond hair sticking out in scouring-pad curls, confiding feminine secrets: "His name is Bobby Jordan, he's a freshman and I think he likes me. It's the perm, I think. It makes me look older."

At fifteen, registering true hórror: "Joey, you're an artist! If you marry Burnett, you'll never forgive yourself. *I'll* never forgive you. It's too grotesque to believe!"

At eighteen, hazel eyes aglow: "His name is Michael Nevis, and I love him, Joey, oh so much..."

At twenty-four, two years ago, sitting in a bright swath of morning sun, her face drawn and vulnerable: "Joey, if Casey had any trouble managing alone, would you help out? And don't give me that nothing's-going-to-happen-to-you look. Sometimes in life, things do happen. Michael's death proved that to me. I want to know that my son will have every chance for love and happiness, whether I'm there or not..."

And in the hospital, just a few months ago, weakened so badly by the virus that had attacked her heart: "This is pointless, I know. But I keep thinking you'll all forget me." The freckles across her nose were barely noticeable, as if her illness had bleached them. "Isn't that silly?"

"No, it's not," Joanna remembered replying, "And we won't forget you. Not ever."

Emily's brave smile had an otherwordly luminosity, "Promise?"

"Promise."

To herself, now, as she held on to Lillian, Joanna silently promised again: We won't forget you, Emily. And we'll make sure that Mike has his chance for all the love and happiness we can give him.

Down in the yard, the song ended. Lillian gave Joanna an extra squeeze, and then pulled away to dash at her damp cheeks with the back of her hand. "Now, give me those pearls. I want to see how they look on you."

Lillian took the necklace, fastening the shining line of diamonds beneath the cluster of dark curls that the hairdresser had let down in back and brushed over one of Joanna's shoulders. "Perfect," she said, when she was done.

Joanna touched the glowing strands. They shone with a rich luster against her skin. "I promise I'll take good care of them."

"Do that," Lillian said. "For the rest of your life."

It took a moment for Lillian's meaning to register. Then Joanna quickly demurred. "Oh, no, Lillian. I couldn't."

"You can and you will. For loving my son, and making him the happiest man in the world at last."

Joanna wanted to cry. The pearls were so beautiful, and yet she felt that taking them would be dishonest. She did love Casey, but not in the way Lillian assumed.

We're doing the right thing, I know we are, she reminded herself silently. Casey and I will have a good life together. It'll work out. It *has* to work out, for Mike's sake.

In the garden below, the pianist had switched to Chopin. Soon, he'd be playing the wedding march. Joanna realized her knees were shaking.

It was really going to happen. She was getting married. To Casey.

Suddenly, it all seemed overwhelming. She, Joanna Vail, artist, a contented and confirmed bachelor by her own definition, was getting married within a matter of minutes.

"Joey? Are you all right?" Lillian's voice came to her.

"Yes," Joanna said, forcing herself to smile. "I'm fine. It's just, you know, wedding day jitters." She glanced at the mirror again, and remembered what she'd been trying to tell Lillian. "And I can't keep the pearls. It wouldn't be right."

"I don't want to hear any more about it." Lillian made her voice stern. "Since it's highly unlikely I'll have another daughter, Casey's wife is the perfect choice for my grandmother's pearls. Now tell me you love them, and you'll treasure them always."

Joanna saw that any further debate would only hurt Lillian, and ruin her joy in presenting such a gift. Resolutely, Joanna pushed away her guilt at letting Lillian think she and Casey were in love. "I adore them," she said. "And I'll treasure them always."

"That's better." Lillian looked content.

Joanna went to the window and gazed out on a cloudless azure sky. The day was perfect for a wedding, sunny, but not too hot. She shifted her gaze downward, to the small gathering of people in the garden.

Beneath a trellis arbor twined with white roses and lilies of the valley, her mother was talking with the minister. Marie glanced up toward the window. Joanna leaned closer to the glass so that her mother could see her. Marie lifted her hand, and Joanna waved back in a signal the two of them had prearranged.

Marie's eager smile was bright as a new day. Joanna smiled back, feeling the tightness of emotion in her chest. Planning a wedding in ten days might be a nerve-racking experience for all concerned, but some good had come of it, too. Joanna felt closer to her mother now than she ever would have thought possible in the years she was growing up.

Joanna turned to Lillian. "Time to go down."

Lillian held out the bouquet of tuberoses and magnolias. Joanna accepted it with a hand that hardly shook at all.

Joanna stood by the side door, thinking vaguely that after this day the scent of tuberoses would always remind her of her wedding day.

The caterer's staff worked quietly by the sink and stove, clinking pans and spoons in a hushed, almost reverent manner. Beyond the kitchen windows, Joanna could see the backs of her friends and family, sitting patiently, waiting for her, the bride, to appear.

The wedding march began, and Joanna left the kitchen to walk up the garden steps to the slate stepping stones that made a natural aisle between the rows of chairs. She heard the muffled rustling as people shifted in their seats to watch her progress. She was aware of their upturned faces, glowing like moons as she passed.

She wondered, is this how every bride feels? Disoriented, floating, numbly abashed that all these people are staring at her?

The minister, a round and smiling man who presided over the church Marie attended, waited beneath the arbor, his face beaming. To the left stood Mike, the only attendant, holding a little tasseled pillow with the rings on it. He was wearing a boy's size cutaway morning coat, with a silk ascot tie and gray striped slacks. He looked very intense, clearly taking the responsibility of his job as ring bearer seriously.

Casey waited in front of the minister. As she moved slowly toward the empty space beside him, Joanna found herself unable to look directly at him. His clothing was identical to Mike's. He was dressed in a gray morning coat and striped slacks, with a white rose in his lapel. The late afternoon sun caught the gold highlights in his hair. Joanna glanced rather desperately over his shoulder, at the beaming minister, at the roses that twined on the arbor, at the clear summer sky, at anything but this man she'd grown up with who would become her husband within a matter of minutes.

The wedding march ended. Joanna was standing at Casey's side. She shot him a nervous, oblique glance and he turned to face the minister with her.

"Dearly beloved, we are gathered here..." the minister began.

Joanna watched the minister's smiling mouth move, and soon she heard the man beside her murmur, "I will."

Then it was her turn. Her voice was surprisingly firm and clear, even clearer than Casey's, she realized with a little flare of pride.

Mike stepped up with the tasseled pillow, and the minister explained the meaning of the rings.

"Like a circle, enclosing your love, infinite and everlasting..."

She looked down at the sprinkling of bronze hairs on the back of Casey's hand as she put the gold band on his finger, and she thought how warm his touch was—and gentle, too—as he slipped her ring in place.

Then the minister said Casey could kiss the bride. Casey put a finger under her chin and tipped her face up, and there was no choice for her but to really look at him.

"Hello, there," he mouthed silently. There were crinkles at the corners of his eyes. He was smiling that smile he always gave her when she was taking herself too seriously—it seemed to say "lighten up." He lifted an eyebrow and she was sure he was thinking the same thing she was; this was going to be their second real kiss.

In recent years, of course, they had often kissed each other. Those little offhand, pecking kisses that you gave someone you cared about when you greeted them, or when you were leaving them. Kisses that missed the person and hit the air around the person's head instead. Hello or see you later or how's-it-going kisses.

Their only real kiss had been fourteen years ago beneath the pines at Graeagle.

And now, here they were, on the verge of their second real kiss, and there were at least forty pairs of eyes watching them. Joanna thought of the innumerable lists her mother had made, and wished she had jotted on one of them, "practice kissing Casey." Because right now, she felt woefully unprepared.

Luckily, Casey seemed willing to meet the challenge. One arm slid to her waist and encircled it, bringing her against him. Since they were almost the same height, they made a surprisingly nice fit, Joanna decided with the objective part of her mind.

She heard a muffled chuckle from somewhere among the guests as Casey's index finger left off propping up her chin to trail down the side of her neck. Lightly, he slipped the finger up under his great-grandmother's antique pearl choker and brought her face close enough to his to get the job done.

Their lips met. His were coaxingly sweet as she somehow knew they would be, or maybe as she remembered them to be so long ago. Joanna's mouth gave under the tender pressure, opening just enough that he subtly traced the inner surface of her lips with a playful tongue. She smiled into the kiss, feeling soft and shy and exceedingly feminine. His arm was firm and supportive at her waist, and his other hand twined seductively in the mass of dark curls at her nape.

She sighed, because it was so lovely. And she totally forgot they had an audience at all until the minister coughed politely.

Casey stopped doing those magical things to her mouth, and stepped away, looping her arm through his. Bemused, she smiled at him. He winked in return, but as subtly as his tongue had teased her lips, so no one else could see. They walked back up the aisle side by side.

Since the wedding was so small and informal, Marie had been persuaded to dispense with a receiving line. Still, once they'd cleared the last row of chairs, Joanna and Casey found themselves surrounded by well-wishers.

She was hugged and kissed. Her back was pounded heartily by one of Casey's flight instructors. The Clinton Airfield office manager, Rhonda Popper, who used a blue rinse on her gray hair and traditionally went to work wearing jogging clothes, had actually worn a dress for the occasion. She grabbed Joanna and commanded with husky fierceness, "You be good to him, you hear?"

"I will," Joanna promised. Over Rhonda's shoulder, Joanna caught a glimpse of raven-black hair and slanted blue eyes. Rhonda stepped away and Althea Gatin took her place.

"You made it. I can hardly believe it." Joanna forced a laugh, dreading the moment when the gallery owner would ask how she was doing on the paintings for the show in September.

Althea bestowed an airy kiss on each of Joanna's cheeks. "I have to keep a watchful eye on my investments, you know." Althea grinned, then murmured in her ear, "I know this isn't the best timing, but I have to get back to L.A. tonight. After the crowd thins out a little, may I have a few moments to go over some business?"

"Sure," Joanna answered promptly, feeling guilty all over again that she'd had no time in the past weeks to think of her work.

"Good," Althea said. "Now, where's the champagne? Weddings always make me thirsty."

Joanna sighed as she watched Althea edge off toward the bar that had been set up down in the lower yard. Before she'd left Los Angeles for Emily's funeral, she'd promised Althea that on her return they'd sit down and make some solid decisions about the theme and scope of her show. But then, she hadn't returned. The few telephone conversations she'd had with Althea since then had been brief, and evasive on her part.

Joanna pushed her neglected work from her mind as the next group of well-wishers stepped up, and Joanna and Casey were again hugged and kissed and congratulated. Finally, the press of people eased—and

Marie closed in. "Time for the pictures," she announced.

Joanna found herself standing again beneath the arbor, being snapped in a variety of groupings for the sake of posterity.

More than one shot included Amanda and Burnett, as immediate family to the groom. The photographer posed Amanda just behind Joanna. As he busied himself placing the subjects and then framing the shot, Amanda whispered tightly into Joanna's ear.

"Joey, aren't those Emily's pearls?"

Joanna was spared a reply by the photographer's command that everybody smile and then his subsequent request for a few more shots of the newlyweds only.

She was soon in Casey's arms again, kissing him for the camera.

"Perfect," said the photographer. "You can stop now."

Joanna, enjoying once again the tender feel of Casey's lips against her own, pulled away with an embarrassed little laugh. Casey lifted his head and she caught a slumberous glint in his eyes, a look that reminded her of the night to come, when they'd be alone together as man and wife for the first time.

That feeling of unreality assailed her again—so much was happening all at once. She was experiencing a kind of emotional vertigo, as if she'd climbed too high too fast and now found herself teetering on the edge of a cliff.

She was *married* to Casey. And tonight, they would do the intimate things that married people did.

It occurred to her that, in all the hustle and bustle to get married, they had never once discussed how they would handle physical intimacy. How in the world could they have forgotten to deal with sex?

Rather frantically, Joanna glanced around the yard, looking for something to focus on, to distract her from further unnerving speculation about her first night as Casey's wife. Her gaze settled on Mike, who was lurking over by the buffet tables, near the wedding cake. He stuck his finger in the frosting and was promptly shooed away by the caterer's assistant.

"Think," Casey said softly, noticing that her eyes were on Mike. "In four years, he'll be the age we were when we first met." He draped an arm across her shoulder. At first she relaxed against him in a comradely way, just as she'd done so many times before. It came to her again that he was her husband now. They were still the same people, yet everything had changed. She didn't move, though her body stiffened slightly. Casey's arm dropped away from her shoulder.

Seeing her opportunity, Althea Gatin approached with one of the flying instructors from the airfield. She patted her escort's arm. "Why don't you and Casey go talk about flight patterns or something. I've got business with the bride."

"Business?" Casey asked. "On our wedding day?"

"Sorry," Althea said. "But your new wife's been a little hard to pin down lately."

Casey laughed. "I understand."

Even through the haze of unreality that had settled over her, Joanna thought he sounded like he really did understand. She reminded herself to be grateful for that. Casey had always taken her work seriously.

She stared after him for a moment, as he walked away with Althea's escort. As he turned his head to speak to his companion, she could see his face in profile. She was impressed by how handsome he was, her new husband... Absurdly, Joanna felt her face flushing.

Althea wasted no time in leading Joanna to a redwood bench in the corner of the yard. "So, how are you doing with my pieces for September?"

Joanna forced her mind to concentrate on business, and cast desperately about for the words to reassure Althea that everything was fine. "I'm working on something...totally different. In fact, I need a little more time before I'll be ready to talk about it."

Althea gave her a glance from those mysteriously slanted eyes, and Joanna knew that the gallery owner hadn't been fooled in the least. "Nothing at all, huh?"

"Things should be settling down here now," Joanna said, wondering how many times she'd used that justification lately. "Then I'll be able to really get some work done."

Althea's sculpted mouth curved upward. "When? During your honeymoon?"

"We aren't taking a honeymoon," Joanna said levelly. Once or twice in the past few days, Casey had dropped some hints about a secluded mountain lodge he knew of in Idaho, but nothing had been agreed upon. Now, as Joanna thought about her career, she decided firmly that they were staying home and she was getting down to work.

"No honeymoon," Althea echoed. "That's a definite?"

"Definite."

"Then you're ready to take on another major commission?"

"What kind of commission?" Joanna stifled an urge to groan aloud, and reminded herself reprovingly that one didn't build a career by turning down work, no matter how behind one was.

"Wall art," Althea answered briskly. "Desert Empire Savings. They've got six branches in Southern California and Arizona. Good money and relatively easy, though the total number of pieces would be considerable."

"Did they ask for me, specifically?"

Althea nodded. "Their representative came into the gallery last week and looked around. Her name is Niki Tori. She felt that those desertscapes you did out at Joshua Tree were stunning—her word and she like the Los Padres Forest series. But her greatest interest was in those three light-and-texture studies. If you ask me, that's the kind of thing she'll be after rather than anything too representational.

"She wants to meet with you, of course." Althea's voice had become far too offhand.

Joanna gave a fatalistic sigh. "You've already set an appointment, haven't you?"

"Nothing ventured—"

"When?"

"August first, a week from this coming Tuesday. Lunch." Althea chuckled wryly. "Lucky you're skipping the honeymoon, isn't it?"

"Very."

"Well?"

"All right. I'll meet with her. But we both know I'm backed up with the show. If she can't give me a reasonable time frame, I'll have to—"

"Don't say it," Althea cut in, only half jokingly. "Wait until you hear the figures. You won't be able to turn it down. And if we have to, we can put off the show."

Joanna rushed to veto that idea. "No, I don't want to do that. It's a big step for me, and I don't want to lose it."

"I didn't say cancel."

"I know what you said. We'd put it off until you have another slot, which could mean a wait of as much as a year. Admit it."

"Joanna, we'll work it out. And stop frowning. You'll get wrinkles before your time."

Joanna said nothing for a moment, only looked down at her satin shoes. When she glanced back up, she'd concluded that the gallery owner was right—and not only about the wrinkles. She'd always known that it wouldn't be easy combining her career with a family. The last week or so she'd told herself that she'd manage it somehow. Some person she'd turn out to be if she went under at the first challenge.

"That's better," Althea said, approving the change in Joanna's expression. "And since you'll be in L.A. for your meeting about the bank commission, we can get down to details on your show once you're through with your negotiations."

"In other words, have something ready by then or else?"

"Well, it would be nice to know what I'm building a whole show out of. Now, I suppose I should let you get back to your wedding day."

"Thanks," Joanna murmured dryly.

"That's quite all right. Where is my flyer?" Althea scanned the yard. "Oh, there he is..." The gallery owner stood up and headed for the buffet tables.

Joanna was left alone on the bench—but not for long. Her Aunt Edna, her mother's sister, soon joined her. Then Nancy, one of Edna's six daughters, strolled over, bringing her own two daughters, and then another aunt, from her father's side of the family. They talked about what a perfect day it was and how wonderful it was that their Joey was at last beginning a family of her own.

She could see Althea and her flyer standing near the bar by the kitchen door. Althea was talking animatedly while her escort was listening.

Joanna couldn't see Casey anywhere.

"Don't you think so, Joanna?" her Aunt Edna was asking.

Joanna brought her attention back to the group of women around her. "I'm sorry. I was thinking of something else. What did you say?"

Aunt Edna smiled knowingly. "Never mind, dear. It's not important."

"If you're looking for Casey, I think I saw him go into the house a few minutes ago," Nancy said.

"Oh, really?" Joanna stood up. "I think I'll go find him."

As she walked away, she could hear her aunts and cousins agreeing on what a beautiful bride she made.

In the house, the kitchen was a beehive of activity, but Casey wasn't there. He wasn't in the big living room, either.

But Amanda was. She hovered near the entrance to the foyer, as if awaiting the signal for a quick getaway.

"Joanna, we were just thinking of leaving," Amanda hastened to explain in a breathless rush, as if she'd been caught doing something reprehensible. "But then Casey and Burnett got into a little discussion."

Dread tightened in Joanna's stomach. For the past ten days, Burnett and his wife had kept a low profile. Joanna had hoped that they might continue to do so—at least until after the wedding. "Where are they?" she asked Amanda.

"Actually, I think they wanted a bit of privacy," Amanda said. "You know how men are."

"What exactly are they discussing, Amanda?"

Amanda glanced nervously around, as if hoping someone would appear to save her from this disagreeable conversation. "Now settle down, Joey. Let's not be hostile."

Joanna remained calm and reasonable. "I'm not hostile, Amanda. I just want to know what's going on."

"Oh, all right." Amanda's attitude of strained propitiation turned to one of resigned acceptance. She tugged Joanna into the shadow of the foyer and spoke in an intimate whisper. "It all started with the pearls," she chided, as if Joanna were a badly behaved child. "You really were naughty to take them, Joey. Those pearls belong in the Clinton family."

Joanna decided against making the obvious arguments: she *was* in the family now. And she hadn't *taken* them; Lillian had given them to her. "What did you do? Corner Lillian and demand to know if she'd given me her grandmother's pearls?"

Amanda's gaze slid guiltily away, then she stuck her chin in the air and said with wounded dignity, "I didn't *demand* anything. I simply asked politely is all."

"And then you went straight to Burnett with the news."

Amanda's eyes glittered like chips of blue ice. "I certainly did. It's bad enough that you and Casey have engineered this fake marriage just so Casey can get his way against Burnett. But when it's all over and Burnett and I have been left to pick up the pieces, I can't bear the thought of you slipping off to Los Angeles with the family jewels."

Joanna didn't know whether to laugh aloud at the twisted workings of Amanda's mind, or to grab the blonde by her delicate shoulders and shake her until her French twist came loose.

Until Emily's death, Joanna had had little opportunity to get to know Burnett's wife. The past weeks had done much to convince her that the less she knew about Amanda Clinton, the better. The woman was like some kind of nightmare Mrs. America, a Princess Grace with fangs.

"Where are they now?" Joanna asked in as civil a tone as she could muster.

"Now, Joey, they want to talk in private."

"I really don't care what they want." Jóanna clasped Amanda's shoulders firmly, impaling her on a stare. "Where are they?"

"Joey, please. You're wrinkling my dress."

"Where?"

"Oh, all right." Amanda gave a weak little shake, and Joanna released her. "Upstairs," Amanda confessed sulkily. "But never tell me I didn't warn you to mind your own business."

"But this *is* my business, Amanda."

"You make everything your business," Amanda accused, her voice low and sibilant. "That's the pushy, unfeminine kind of woman you are."

"I'm sorry you feel that way, Amanda."

"Oh no you're not. You don't care how anybody feels, just as long as you get your way."

Joanna left Burnett's wife wearing a disdainful pout and smoothing the silk of her sleeve.

She was already on the stairs when Marie called to her from the door to the kitchen. "Joanna, there you are." Joanna watched her mother approach, followed by Lillian. "Everyone's asking where the bride and groom have gone off to." Marie bustled up, Lillian close behind. Both women stood at the foot of the stairs and looked up at her expectantly.

Joanna hesitated in midstep. "I think Casey's upstairs with Burnett," she explained, eager to be gone. "I was just going to find him." She started to rush up the stairs again.

Her mother's voice stopped her. "Joanna? Is something wrong?" A worried frown had creased Marie's forehead. She'd begun to suspect that something disturbing was going on. "Joanna? What is it?"

"Nothing. Really." Joanna tried to keep her expression composed as she decided her next move. The last thing she wanted was to lead the two women in the middle of a fight. But, on the other hand, it was too late to insist that they stay behind without further worrying Marie.

Well, she finally reasoned rather desperately, when in doubt, do something. Joanna gulped and beamed a thousand watt smile at her mother. "Why don't you two come help me drag them back down to the party?"

"Certainly." The deep worry lines in Marie's forehead eased. "Come on, Lillian." Marie was already bustling up the stairs.

Chapter Four

When she reached the top step, Joanna could hear muffled masculine voices in the bedroom off the stairwell.

Without a pause, she swept into the room. "There you two are!" Her voice was absurdly breathy. "I've been looking all over for you."

Burnett, who was facing the far wall, turned and glowered. Casey, slouched in an armchair, lifted an eyebrow at her and then gave a low chuckle when he saw Marie and Lillian behind her.

Lillian stayed near the door wearing a pleasant, neutral smile. Marie, on the other hand, seemed to have assessed the situation at a glance. She bustled into the room. "Come along, now, Casey," Marie clucked. "Your guests are feeling neglected." She gave

Burnett one of her best hostess smiles. "You two don't mind continuing your little talk later. Do you?"

Burnett said nothing for a moment, and Joanna found herself waiting fatalistically for the ax to fall. But when he spoke, it was in a perfectly civil tone.

"No, of course not. Amanda and I have to be going anyway." Confronted by his hostess, the bride and his own mother, he'd obviously decided it would be in bad taste to continue fighting with the groom.

"Oh. So soon?" Marie said. Joanna glanced sharply at her mother, whose expression was too guileless to believe.

"Yes, I'm afraid so," Burnett answered in a tone of feigned regret. He nodded at his brother. "Casey."

Wryly, Casey saluted him.

"Goodbye, Joanna," Burnett said with the strained nobility of a king being polite to one of the palace serving girls.

Joanna nodded, though she needn't have bothered. The tall, imposing figure was already passing Lillian at the door.

"We'll see them out," Marie announced, taking Lillian's arm and starting for the stairs. She turned briefly to her daughter and new son-in-law. "Come along, you two. You'll have a lifetime to be alone together. But now, your guests are waiting."

Casey uncurled from his chair and approached Joanna.

"What happened?" she asked.

He shook his head. "More of the same. We can talk about it tonight, after all this is over."

Joanna decided he was right, now was not the time.

"I think I'm ready for champagne," she said. "About a barrelful."

Casey took her arm and they descended the stairs to rejoin the party.

In the yard, the shadows grew longer as evening approached. The rituals of the wedding day continued, one after the other.

Joanna and Casey ate together at one of the small round tables that had been set up near the buffet. They cut the cake and fed each other sugary slices for the photographer's benefit. They drank champagne from each other's glasses, elbows linked, as her Aunt Edna's husband, Uncle Nathan, proposed toast after toast:

"To Life.

"To Health.

"To Love.

"To Happiness..."

And after darkness fell and the aisles of folding chairs had been cleared away, they danced on the lawn in the upper yard as a sliver of moon smiled down on them.

Joanna had always liked dancing with Casey. He knew how to lead, but he never made his partner aware that he was doing so. Joanna gave herself over to the music, a blissful lassitude invading her limbs.

"Nice," she sighed.

He made a low answering sound and pulled her closer.

The champagne was really doing the trick, she decided. "I think everything's going to be fine," she murmured in his ear. "As Uncle Nathan pointed out, we're alive and we're healthy. We love each other, um, in our own way. So I think this must be happiness I'm feeling right now."

"*I* think you're feeling about four glasses of champagne."

"You're right," she said. "It's a bubbly kind of happiness. And I like it very much. I hope it never ends."

"Is that what you'll say in the morning?"

"No, in the morning, I'll probably say, 'where's the aspirin?'"

His low chuckle stirred her hair as he pulled her close again.

An hour later, Joanna stood on the staircase and tossed her bouquet. Althea, who'd been married more than once already, snatched it from the air. "Oh, no!" The gallery owner's trilling laugh rang out. "Not again..."

A cousin of Casey's caught the garter and promptly displayed it on his sleeve.

Mike had fallen asleep on the living-room floor and Rhonda Popper had carried him up to one of the bedrooms. Casey and Joanna went to get him. They found him sleeping on his stomach in his T-shirt and slacks. Rhonda had thoughtfully seen to the removal of his coat, shirt and shoes. His head was turned to the side, his mouth open.

"Down for the count," Casey said softly. "I wish I didn't have to disturb him."

Casey scooped up his nephew and settled the boy's head on his shoulder. Mike's stockinged feet dangled below Casey's waist. His red-blond hair stood straight up from his head where he'd lain on it.

"He doesn't look too bothered," Joanna remarked, as Mike gave a sleepy little snort and snuggled more comfortably into the curve of Casey's neck.

Casey captured her gaze over Mike's tousled head. As always, his crooked grin charmed her.

Joanna grinned back, thinking that the happiness of the rumpled child in Casey's arms was well worth the chaos of all the changes occurring in their lives.

"Let's go home," Casey said.

Joanna turned and led the way.

Mike slept through the congratulatory goodbyes, through being strapped into the back seat of the car, and even through the ride home, a noisy experience because of the clanging rattle of the cans that one of Casey's friends had tied to the muffler.

They put him to bed in his room without even undressing him, and he crawled beneath the covers, not really waking except to mutter, "Can we have waffles tomorrow, to celebrate?"

"You bet, now back to sleep." Joanna tugged the blankets up around him and settled him in. Then she and Casey left him to his dreams.

They went upstairs, talking softly about the day's events. It seemed perfectly natural for them to go to Casey's room.

Casey flicked on the two lamps by the bed, and the sparsely furnished space glowed with subtle light. When Casey had first shown her the room, four years ago, Joanna had been intrigued. Its spareness had surprised her. Before, Casey's taste had always run to the "tacky-sexy," as she used to tease him. He'd liked intense colors and water beds. But this room was different. Perhaps it reflected a more mature Casey.

The walls and ceiling were painted off-white. The big bed had a black iron frame, its four slender black posts capped with lethal looking spiked finials. The bed linen was creamy white, but the throw covers across the foot resembled a Moorish tapestry, in blood red, mustard and black. The short, close-woven carpet was the color of tanned leather, and the bedstands and chests were of dark, rich mahogany.

A pair of Tuscan mahogany columns defined a sitting area, which contained a small cinnamon-brown leather couch, two armchairs and a mother-of-pearl inlaid mahogany trunk that doubled as a low table. Like Joanna's room across the landing, this room had two large bay windows, one behind the couch and the other on the adjacent wall. There was also a whimsical round window, high above the bed, which Joanna had loved on sight. In the daytime, it let in a leaf-shadowed disc of sunlight that moved around the room as the hours advanced.

Joanna slipped out of her shoes and settled into one of the armchairs, immediately drawing her legs up under the diaphanous fabric of her dress. She felt utterly at ease. Her nervousness about the time when they'd finally be alone together as man and wife had faded away. Now that the moment was actually here, she recognized the absurdity of her fears. After all, they were still the same two people, best friends since childhood. On the deepest level, nothing had really changed.

Casey, however, seemed a little on edge. He prowled the room, shrugging out of his jacket, getting rid of his ascot and unbuttoning the wing collar of his stiff, starched shirt.

When he sat on the edge of the bed and shucked off his shoes, he appeared to relax. A smile played on his lips as they spoke of Marie's take-charge behavior with Burnett.

"I never thought I'd say this," he remarked after she'd told him how Marie and Lillian had caught her on the stairs. "But I think I could get to like your mother."

"Know what? I think I could, too."

"You've...explained the situation to her?" Casey asked. Joanna didn't miss the hesitation in the question. It meant he didn't like what he assumed she'd done, but was willing to be understanding about it.

The happy haze of contentment she'd found with the help of the champagne thinned a little. When she'd agreed to marry Casey, they'd decided it was important that everyone think they were marrying for love. That way, Burnett could never tell a judge that their union wasn't a real one. Now Casey was accusing her of telling her mother that they'd only married for Mike's sake. Joanna didn't like the implication that she couldn't keep her part of their bargain. "What situation do you mean, exactly?"

He stood up, his shoes in his hand. His quick glance at her was very tolerant, irritatingly so. "Don't be defensive."

"I'm not."

"Joey." He stood up, circled the bed and put the shoes away in the closet. Then he slid the door closed. "I can understand if you felt you had to tell your mother that we were doing all this to keep Burnett from getting Mike.''

''She doesn't know.''

He came to her side of the room and dropped into the chair opposite her. ''Joey, we *have* to stay honest with each other, or this isn't going to work.''

His self-righteous tone rankled. ''I *am* being honest.''

He kept looking at her, unbelieving. ''I know your mother. She's too self-absorbed to be that perceptive on her own.''

Never in her life would Joanna have imagined that she'd be defensive of Marie. But she was now. ''Thank you very much. And what about *your* mother? She's still standing around with a vacant smile on her face while her sons tear at each other's throats—''

Casey stepped back as if she'd slapped him.

''I'm sorry,'' Joanna said quietly, ashamed of herself. ''That was fighting dirty. I love Lillian, you know that.''

''I know.'' Casey sprawled backward with a sigh, laying his hands on each arm of the chair. He looked up at the ceiling. ''She's always tried not to take sides.''

''I can understand that,'' Joanna conceded. ''But, in this case, Mike's future is at stake.''

''Tell me about it. But my mother is my mother. She's dealt with Burnett and me in the same way ever since I can remember. She's not likely to change now.''

''I think it's sad,'' Joanna said. ''To be such a great lady and then to have this one huge blind spot.''

''Welcome to the human race.''

Joanna realized he was waiting for her to explain exactly what she'd told her mother.

"All right," she said. "As far as what I told my mother—"

He chuckled. "Going to make a clean breast of it, huh?" His tone was blessedly light.

She entered into the banter with a feeling of relief. "If you make one more snide remark, I will tell you nothing. Nothing. Do you understand?"

"God, you're tough."

"It's true. I can be ruthless. So shut up and listen."

"Yes, ma'am."

"I *did* tell my mother that Burnett is angry because Emily left Mike with you. She'd be likely to find that out eventually anyway, and she'd only be hurt if she thought I hadn't trusted her enough to tell her myself. But as for the rest, we agreed to let everyone think we're in love." Joanna's tone lost its bantering lightness. She looked away from him, toward the mean looking finials on the white bed. "I'm doing my best."

"Hey." His single coaxing word hung on the air for a moment, and then she looked at him again. "I apologize for doubting you."

"It's all right." She let her gaze drift upward, to the round window above the bed. The branches of a live oak touched the glass outside, as if scratching to come in from the dark. She looked down again and idly began undoing the long row of tiny buttons on her sleeve.

"Tired?" Casey asked.

One by one, the buttons slipped from their holes. "A little, I guess. And sort of deflated."

"Come here," Casey said.

He held out his hand and she reached across to put hers in it. He gave a tug. She left her own chair and dropped onto the arm of his.

His gaze roved her face. "Even if she's not in love, the bride is beautiful," he said. "And the groom's a fortunate man."

"Thanks, pal." She lifted her arms and began to remove the silk flowers woven into her hair. "Now tell me what happened with Burnett."

He watched the movement of her hands. She thought his gaze strayed down once or twice to where her dress clung closely to her breasts, responding to the movement of her lifted arms. As she slowly removed the adornments in her hair she realized he didn't make her uncomfortable at all. It seemed the most natural thing, as if it had always been that way. The two of them, talking over the events of the day, getting ready for bed.

"There's nothing much to tell," he said. "It was just more of the same."

She stretched out her arm to set the sprays of cloth flowers and the pearl clip on the mahogany chest and then settled back close to him, tugging on one of the points of his collar. "Come on. What did he say?"

Casually, Casey stroked the ropes of pearls at her neck, causing them to roll against her skin. She smiled, enjoying the feeling of being caressed by pearls. "He was angry about these," Casey said.

She reached behind her and unfastened the gleaming strands. "I know that. I talked to Amanda. She wasn't happy when she learned that your mother had given them to me."

"Amanda is a menace," Casey said.

She handed him the pearls, and her mother's pearl hair clip. "Do you have a place you could put these?" He nodded and went to lay them in a small jewel case inside a bureau drawer.

He came back to the chair they'd been sharing, sat down and began winding a corkscrew of her hair around his finger. "I think, though, that the necklace was only an excuse." As he played with her hair, his expression became almost dreamy. "Burnett just wanted another opportunity to tell me he's going to be waiting for this marriage of ours to start falling apart." He pulled his finger from a shining curl and his voice grew somewhat brisk. "Which, in reality, means that he's talked to his lawyer and been told that he doesn't have much of a chance as long as I'm a married man. Now he has nothing to offer Mike that I can't offer. Less, actually, when you add Emily's own wishes, as stipulated in her will."

"Plus love and happiness, don't forget those," Joanna hastened to add.

Casey's face grew serious. "I haven't forgotten. Not for a minute."

Joanna stared into his light-filled eyes, and then she looked at his mouth. Down in the womanly center of her, something warm happened, a tiny fluttering, like a promise of desire. She wanted to explore it, coax it to grow stronger. But she was scared, too, because it reminded her that the axis of their friendship was changing—like a planet being tilted in the heavens by some new gravitational force. She feared what might happen, feared spinning wildly out of her known orbit, into empty space.

"Casey?" Her hand was on his chest, which was warm and solid beneath the stiff dress shirt.

"Yes?" he said.

It seemed the most natural thing to run her hand lightly over the round pectoral muscles that she could feel beneath his shirt. "You don't regret this, do you?"

"No." He sounded very sure. He traced the tip of her chin with the pad of his thumb. "Do you?"

"No, but—"

"But what?"

She couldn't help it. She moved her head closer, so that she could feel his gentle breath against her mouth. "It's all changing. And it scares me. And then again..."

"Yes?"

"Sometimes I like it. Sometimes I wonder..."

"Go on."

When she turned her head slightly, he captured her chin and made her keep looking at him.

"Sometimes you wonder what?" he asked.

She looked into his eyes and wondered again. The question had been in the back of her mind for a while now. It occurred to her especially at night when she slept alone, when her mind went its own way and started thinking of their past.

"What would have happened if," she whispered.

His mouth was so close, his eyes lit with that same languid intent that had burned in them when he'd kissed her for the photographs, beneath the arbor in the bright sunlight.

"What would have happened if what?"

"If you'd done more than kiss me fourteen years ago..."

His lips, breath-close, curled slightly upward. "We'll never know." The fingers that had captured her chin stroked downward, skimming the line of her neck.

So marvelously strange. He'd touched no part of her that he hadn't touched a hundred times as her friend, and yet every touch was a discovery, brimful with shimmering and intimate intent.

He took a curling tendril of her hair that fell over her shoulder and lightly tugged it.

That brought her mouth down to his. "How about if we concentrate on what's happening right now?"

She kissed him on the word "now," tasting him teasingly, lightly, on a side to side movement as his breath whispered across her mouth. "All right."

The kiss deepened. He put a coaxing hand at her waist and she slid easily off the arm of the chair and into his lap.

The kiss went on and on, delicious and exploratory, as she felt his hands caressing her through the frothy material of her dress. His touch molded the round line of her hip, defined the long curve of thigh to her knee and then back up again. It was a questing touch, one that refused to be hurried.

Joanna shifted against his chest, wishing she could just melt right into him. She swept her arms up to encircle his neck so she could press herself more closely into his body.

And then he touched her breast.

It was a caressing, exploring touch, no different than the feel of his hands on the rest of her body.

But still, immeasurably different. It was the place they'd stopped so long ago, beneath the pines behind the cabin that weekend he'd kidnapped her to keep her from marrying his brother.

A turning point. Her heart seemed to lift and hover high up in her chest—because the invisible line was being bridged. They were approaching ground on which they'd never before trod together.

His touch burned through the sheer dress and through the wisps of silk below, unbearably intimate. In its cradle of lace, her nipple grew hard, blooming out toward his palm. Could he feel her body's readying response, through all the layers of bridal adornment that separated his flesh from hers?

Joanna froze, a tiny confused sound escaping her. Without even thinking about it, she jerked back and met his eyes. They burned into hers, knowing her.

It was scary how well he knew her. Naked before him, she would be so much more naked than before any other man.

"I— I'm not sure I'm ready for this," she got out on a shaky breath.

"I know." His voice held that huskiness that came from arousal, but his gaze was level. His cradling hand had already left her breast.

He swung her up against his chest as he stood up.

She laughed, the sound high and unsure. "Casey, what are you doing?"

"Putting you to bed."

Joanna looped her arms around his neck and buried her face in his collar, thinking that it would work out all right, steeling herself for the scariness of the coming intimacy in his big white bed.

Since her eyes were closed, she didn't realize that he wasn't carrying her to *his* bed until he nudged open the door to the landing with his foot. He took her to her own room and put her down on her feet in the middle of the floor.

"Stay there," he said, and went around the big room, rolling up the blinds until the space was softly lit with the glow from the street lamps beyond the windows. Then he approached the neat little daybed, took the bolsters off and drew back the spread and covers.

Joanna watched him, saying nothing, but thinking that the bed was awfully small for two when they had his big one in the room they'd just left. But then, maybe he thought she'd feel more comfortable here, in her own territory.

She decided not to mention her doubts about the bed. He was being thoughtful, she wouldn't ruin it for him. Besides, her silly heart was pounding harder by the minute. If she dared to speak, she felt her heart might leap out of her mouth and dance around the dimly lit room.

He returned to her. "Hold out your hand."

She did. With great care, he unbuttoned her sleeve. "The other one."

It was the one she'd already started, so he made short work of it.

Then he smoothly and efficiently undid the front buttons, opening the airy fabric and slipping it over her shoulders, catching it before it touched the floor. He carried the dress to the closet and hung it inside.

Joanna stood in her ivory silk braslip, waiting, until he returned.

"What do you want to wear?" he asked, still standing by the open closet.

She blinked, confused. "Pardon me?" She felt her whole body flushing, and was glad for the dimness of the light.

"To bed."

"Oh, nothing," she answered. In summer, she rarely wore much to bed. But then she felt absurdly forward, and yet inept at the same time, so she added, "Just this slip, I guess."

She stared down at the lace-trimmed hem of that slip for a minute, realizing that it had never even occurred to her in the past weeks to buy a sexy nightgown for this landmark occasion. But then she decided it didn't matter. The way things were progressing Casey would be dressing her in it only to take it right off again.

He slid the closet door shut and started to walk toward her again. Quickly, she slithered out of her pantyhose, not sure she could bear having him help her out of them.

He held out his hand. Not sure exactly what he wanted, she dropped the panty hose in it. The wisp of nylon fell across his palm. He looked down at it, then glanced back at her with his crooked grin. He turned, and draped them across the chair by the closet.

She waited. He held out his hand again. Hesitantly, she laid hers in it.

"Come on," he said. "Get into bed." He pulled her toward the turned-down daybed. She followed his lead, climbing between the covers and lying there quietly while he pulled them up under her arms.

Then he sat on the side of the bed. "Sleep well, Joey."

She realized then that he wasn't going to stay. And she experienced disappointment, mingled with relief. "This *is* our wedding night," she told him softly.

"We need to give it time."

"Chicken."

"No dares, Joey, okay? Not about this. You were the one who said everything's happening so fast. This is something we have control over. We don't have to be pushed into this too fast, just because it's our wedding night. This is the one thing in all of this that can be just between you and me. We can set a pace that's right for both of us."

"I suppose you're right," she allowed, though she felt out of sorts. The way he was leaving her now seemed another example of how strange things had become. He always seemed to be leaving the room at crucial moments, with nothing ever settled, with things always somehow up in the air.

"I know I'm right," he was saying. He stood up. "Good night, Joey."

"Good night," she heard herself answer. He left her, softly pulling her door shut behind him.

Joanna lay alone in her single bed on her wedding night and wondered what in the world was happening.

Remembering what had just transpired, she felt again the lovely, cradling touch of his hand on her breast, felt her nipple rising, blooming in its nest of lace.

It would have been all right, she was sure. It would have been fine if they'd gone on to fulfillment. But

Casey had stopped it, using her slight hesitation as an excuse.

She wondered if he was having trouble getting aroused. They were, after all, best friends, with twenty-two years of strictly platonic closeness between them. Maybe when it came down to sex, Casey was realizing he wanted things to stay platonic.

Joanna didn't like to think that Casey could be finding it difficult to desire her, especially because she was finding it so effortless to desire him. Her body thrummed with unsatisfied anticipation.

They should talk about it, she decided.

She was out of the daybed and halfway to the door before her courage deserted her.

Things had changed between them in the past week and a half. So much of the old easy camaraderie was gone. She realized that to barge into his room in the middle of the night wearing only a slip to ask him if he found the idea of sex with her repugnant called for more nerve than Joanna possessed.

Besides that, the calming effects of the champagne she'd drunk at the wedding had worn off. She was left with a dull headache and a raging thirst.

Joanna detoured to the bathroom, where she washed down two aspirin with several glasses of tap water. Behind the door, her paint-spattered work shirt hung on a hook.

The idea of working suddenly had great appeal—especially when considering the alternatives of trying to sleep or seeking Casey out.

Joanna put on the shirt. Then she returned to the other room and took a sketch pad and a few sticks of charcoal from the long folding table that held her supplies. She carried them to the window seat that overlooked the front lawn and made herself comfortable.

She reached over to the black gooseneck lamp that craned over her drawing table and adjusted it to shine down on the sketch pad in her lap.

She flipped open the cover and stared at a blank page.

She had no idea what would take shape there, no idea at all. And for a while, nothing did. For a while, she just sat, very still, her eyes focused out the window on the street where Casey lived, the street that was now where she lived, too.

And then her hand, clutching the stick of charcoal, began to move across the pad.

A soft smile on her lips, Joanna glanced out the window. The street lights suddenly went off, and an enterprising young girl on a bicycle passed along the sidewalk, pitching fat Sunday papers onto front driveways from a huge wire bin attached to her handlebars.

Dawn, Joanna thought, and shook her head. She'd spent her entire wedding night sitting alone alternately staring out the window and sketching out hasty renderings of whatever popped into her head. She looked down at the sketch pad. It was flipped to the last sheet.

Slowly, with growing excitement, she thumbed through the pages. Each one was filled with sketches.

By the growing light of dawn, Joanna knew what the sketches meant. They were a message from her creative self, that part of her so scarily silent for the past few weeks.

She had her theme for September's show. It was going to be families—hers and Casey's. And she would call the whole thing Family Album.

She would have several studies of Emily, from childhood to adulthood. She would show Mike, half-dressed in his formal attire as a ring bearer, asleep in her mother's upstairs bedroom. She'd have her own mother, talking to the minister beneath the arbor yesterday. And Burnett, at about fifteen, at Chilly Lilly's in that paper hat he used to wear when he worked behind the counter.

There were a thousand scenes for her to choose from, Joanna realized, and in her Los Angeles apartment were some already completed studies of Emily and a few posed portraits of Mike. She could show those to Althea next week, if she didn't get anything new ready before then.

Joanna set aside the sketch pad and headed for the door, her stomach fluttering with excitement. She wanted to tell Casey. He'd be so excited.

Chapter Five

He was sleeping half-under, half-out of the covers, wearing only a pair of white cotton briefs. Joanna closed the door very softly and crept to the side of the bed.

He really was a beautiful man, she decided, the artist in her still thrumming with purpose and exhilaration. Really physically beautiful, and almost as beautiful on the outside as in his spirit and heart.

She wished she'd brought her sketch pad.

She stood in pure sensual appreciation of him, not wanting to disturb the picture of male beauty in repose.

One tanned, lean foot lay in a relaxed pose on top of the sheet. She gazed at it, at the good bones, the high arch, the gleam of health and strength in the brown skin, the sprinkling of hairs across the toes and instep.

Her appreciative gaze glided upward, over a lean ankle, a hard bulge of calf, and the good, clear bones in the knee, all dusted with gleaming, wiry brown hair.

The three long, wrapping muscles of his thigh were pure poetry, braiding in smooth bulges beneath his golden skin up to the whiteness of his briefs and a clot of wrinkled sheet.

He held the sheet against his belly. His flanks showed hard muscle, the stomach slightly rippled in that lovely "washboard" effect. Crisp hair grew thickest in a trail up the solar plexus line and separated out into little whorls at the pectorals.

Her gaze tracked out and down again, over a golden bulge of deltoid muscle at the shoulder, to well-defined triceps and biceps, and good radials beneath the elbow.

"Have I got my shorts on backward or something?" Casey's drowsy voice made Joanna jump like a naughty child who'd been caught snatching forbidden cookies. Her glance shot up to his face. His eyes were half-open, watching her, and a lazy smile was on his lips.

She took an unconscious step back, felt a bedside chair against her knees, and dropped into it. "I had this idea..." she managed lamely, and then felt disgusted with herself. It was much more than just an *idea*. "Scratch that," she amended, "It was an inspiration, a *revelation!*"

He sat up and stretched. "And all before even one cup of coffee?"

"I was up all night. Thinking and sketching."

"And?"

"I've got it," she said, taking pleasure in drawing out her excitement. It was nice, she thought, to have someone to share a breakthrough with. "It's families. Our families."

"Great," he said. "Now translate."

"You know Althea's promised me my own show in September?"

"I remember you mentioning something to that effect."

"Well, she caught me yesterday and wanted to pin me down on what I'm planning to do for it. And I still couldn't tell her a thing, because I didn't have a thing. Furthermore, she told me I've got to meet a big potential client next week to discuss wall art for a bank chain."

"You didn't tell me that last night."

"I forgot. I mean, we had all those other things to talk about and well, maybe I didn't want to think about it because I was scared to death I was in way over my head."

He arched an eyebrow at her. "And are you?"

She grinned smugly. "Not anymore. Like I said, I've got it."

"Families, right?" he said, still not understanding.

"My big show. It's going to be the Clintons and the Vails. I've been thinking and sketching all night and I know just what I'm going for and how to go about getting it." In her enthusiasm, she shot off the chair and jumped onto the bed beside him. "Only I can't tell you that part, not in detail. You know that. That would take the punch out of it, to talk it to death." She stretched out, face down across the foot of the bed, all her tired muscles seeming to sigh and groan at once. "Oh, I'm exhausted. Just wrung out from being brilliant all night long."

He chuckled. "And so unassuming, too."

She rolled over and wrinkled her nose. "False modesty has never been my long suit." Idly, she combed her tangled hair out over the edge of the bed with her fingers, and then she noticed that the tips of her fingers were black with charcoal. "I'm a mess, huh?"

"Brilliance always has its price."

"Slick, Clinton," she shot back. "Very slick." She grinned at him, full of euphoric enthusiasm. She was so excited about her breakthrough that she'd almost managed to forget about the changes that were happening between the two of them.

"Why do I get the feeling this is going to put a crimp in my big surprise?" he asked.

Joanna looked up at him. "You have a surprise?"

He nodded. "I already made arrangements for Mother to take Mike. And you and I were leaving today, as a matter of fact."

"For where?"

"Would you believe Puerto Vallarta?"

"Mexico?"

"Last I checked, that's where they put Puerto Vallarta. I've been picturing us deep-sea fishing, and windsurfing."

"But it's tropical!" The words escaped her lips before she considered how critical they sounded. "I mean, right now I can't be anywhere tropical. It's completely wrong."

He looked hurt. "Thanks."

She wriggled upright and sat on her heels. "Oh, Casey. I'm sorry. I didn't mean it like that. I just meant that the stuff I'll be working on now won't have a tropical feel at all. It would set the wrong mood altogether."

"I see." He didn't look as if he saw at all.

"And besides, there's my meeting next week."

"Right. About the banks."

Joanna looked down at her hands, all smudged with charcoal, which she'd folded on her thighs. "I'm sorry. I should have told you last night that we'd have to postpone a honeymoon."

"It's okay," he said. "I knew when we decided to get married that your work would always be a consideration in any decision. It's no problem. I'll call Mother and tell her she's off the hook for baby-sitting. And tell you what? Maybe Mike and I will fly to L.A. with you."

"I'll bet you cleared your schedule at the airfield and everything." Casey taught flying and oversaw the entire operation. Though his schedule was flexible, he still needed to spend a lot of time at work. To have arranged for more than a week off would not have been an easy matter.

"Will you stop feeling guilty about being who you are?" Casey sounded as if he might be losing patience.

Joanna decided he had a point. "You're right. I'm not a conventional person—and this isn't a conventional marriage."

"That's better." He swung his legs over the side of the bed and stood up. Joanna's hands itched for a stick of charcoal and her sketch pad. A few of her new pieces would have Casey as the subject. Right now, as he walked away from her, the broad line of his back, tapering into his waist and down to hard hips was something to see. Also, his gluteals were nothing to sneeze at—from a purely aesthetic point of view, of course.

Unaware of her scrutiny, Casey went to the mahogany dresser and pulled out some gray sweats. He shoved his legs into them and tied them at the waist. Then he caught her watching him. He froze, and stared right back at her.

Joanna gulped, remembering how she'd almost paid him a visit in the middle of the night to talk about sex. Maybe now, in the bright light of day, in nonthreatening circumstances would be a good time to broach the subject.

"What?" he asked, as if cuing her.

"Hey, Joey! Uncle Case..." Mike stood in the doorway, dangling a balsa wood glider from one hand and still wearing his striped dress slacks from the day before. He looked from his uncle to Joanna and back again, sensing, as children often do, that he'd interrupted at an awkward moment.

"Ever heard of knocking?" Casey asked wryly.

"The door was half-open."

Joanna glanced at Casey and nodded. "I left it that way when I came in." She looked at Mike again. "It's all right. Come on in."

Mike looked doubtful for a moment, and then he crossed the threshold. "I'm starved."

"For waffles?" Joanna asked.

"Yep." He looked at Joanna's smeared hands. "But you better wash your hands first, Joey."

"She better wash her whole self," Casey winked at Joanna. "Go on. Take a shower. We'll get things moving on the waffle front." He scooped up a giggling Mike and set him on his shoulders. "Come on, kid. Let's split this scene." They were at the door already. "Duck," Casey ordered, and Mike did.

Joanna stood still for a moment, listening with pleasure to the childish voice and the deeper one, laughing and talking as they went down the stairs.

She felt a twinge of regret—for what hadn't quite been said before Mike burst in. But then she turned her mind back to her work and decided that time would take care of the problems between Casey and herself.

Casey called Lillian right after breakfast and told her they were staying home after all. Then he went about canceling their reservations.

By noon, Joanna's lack of sleep had caught up with her. They were out by the pool, and Casey ordered her upstairs when he caught her snoozing on her air mattress. She slept until dinner, which was barbecued ribs and corn on the cob eaten outside on the picnic table.

Once Mike was in bed, they sat outside for a while as the night grew darker. Joanna felt the urge to work again, like a strong thread pulling her upstairs where her drawing board, pastels, charcoal and paints waited.

Casey rolled his head over to her from the chaise longue next to hers and said. "Go on. Go to it."

"Would you mind?" Her voice was sheepish.

"I said get lost." He turned his head back toward the stars and closed his eyes.

"Georgia O'Keefe and her husband lived separately." She mentioned a contemporary artist famous for her vivid paintings of desert flowers and animal skulls. "He stayed in New York and she lived in Arizona."

"Are you trying to make a point?"

"Just that it could be worse." Her voice held a sheepish note.

He still had his eyes closed, his face turned to the sky. "I didn't hear myself complaining. Was I complaining?"

"No, I was feeling guilty."

"Again?"

"I'm sorry."

"Are you still here?"

She rose quietly from the lawn chair and went to her studio.

And the night, again, slipped by in a magic haze of creative work.

At dawn, she showered and was on her way to Casey's room to wake him up, when another idea came to her, one she had to get down. She worked for another couple of hours, and then she smelled coffee.

Joanna followed her nose downstairs and straight to the coffeemaker that sat on the counter by the front window. She tossed a vague smile at Casey and Mike as she passed them. The boy and the man were sitting at a breakfast bar formed by a section of counter that projected into the room. They were surrounded by boxes of cold cereal.

Casey read the paper as he spooned shredded wheat into his mouth. Mike, Joanna's cursory glance revealed, was pouring something called Boffo Balls into his bowl, a cereal blinding in its brightness. Round balls in pink, yellow, green and blue tumbled out of the box.

Joanna poured her coffee.

"Joey, I think you should start sleeping at night again. You don't look so good," Mike said from behind her. She could hear milk sloshing into his bowl.

"Um," Joanna murmured. Out the window, she was watching a white station wagon pull up to the curb. Amanda Clinton emerged from it and came up the front walk. Joanna suddenly wished she could turn around, mount the stairs again, climb into her daybed and pull the covers over her head.

Chapter Six

Amanda stood at the door clutching a bag with a famous designer's initials all over it. "Hello, Joey." Her delft-blue eyes scanned Joanna's torn jeans, her rumpled work shirt and her wild, uncoiffed hair.

Amanda's bowed lips formed a slight moue of distaste, which she quickly banished. "Lillian said you weren't going on a trip after all, so I thought I would drop by this morning before my Women's Auxilliary meeting at the hospital." Amanda mentioned one of her numerous volunteer affiliations at normal volume, then she lowered her voice to a subdued murmur. "I think we need to get a few things cleared up, don't you—for little Mike's sake, if for no other reason."

Joanna longed to remind Amanda of that handy little device known as the telephone, and to add that she personally liked to be warned before hostile in-laws came calling at 8:30 a.m. But she didn't. Amanda was right, they did need to learn to get along with each other.

"Come in," Joanna said. "Want some coffee?"

"Yes, thank you."

Joanna led her to the kitchen, where she poured coffee for her new sister-in-law while Mike greeted her around a mouthful of Boffo Balls.

"'Morning, Amanda." Casey glanced at Joanna. Joanna nodded imperceptibly, signaling that nothing was happening that she couldn't handle. Casey returned to his paper.

"What kind of breakfast is this for a growing boy?" Amanda picked up the cereal box and began reading the ingredients on the side. "Joanna, the second ingredient is sugar."

"That's why he likes it so much," Casey remarked from behind the sports section.

Amanda clucked her tongue. "I suppose it's none of my business, but . . ."

Casey reached out and took the box away from her. "You're right, Amanda. It's none of your business." He set the box back on the counter with a smart thump.

"Well, pardon me." Amanda clutched her designer bag more tightly.

From behind his paper, Casey only grunted. Mike, wise beyond his years, said nothing, but went on contentedly crunching his sugar-packed breakfast.

Joanna slid around the end of the breakfast bar, carrying a small tray with two full cups and cream and sugar on it. "Why don't we go out back. It's such a beautiful morning, after all." She kept her voice purposely light and cheerful.

"Certainly," Amanda sniffed, and followed her out to sit beside the pool.

They sat across from each other beneath the umbrella at the round table, Joanna facing the pool and Amanda facing the house. Amanda blew lightly on her coffee before she sipped from it. Then she sat back in the padded chair, holding her cup in both hands.

"As you know," she began after a moment, "Burnett and I are quite distressed at what is happening in this family."

Amanda paused, as if waiting for Joanna to make some affirmative comment. To spur her on, Joanna said, "Oh?"

"And of course we all know what is going to happen in the end." She paused again. Joanna assumed she was expected to ask "What?" But she didn't.

Amanda frowned at the lack of response and continued. "But I suppose there's nothing to be gained by belaboring the obvious, so I'll get to the reason I came this morning." She paused again, but Joanna was just exasperated enough to be through making polite noises.

"We're going to have to *try* to get along, Joey. For Mike's sake. And of course, for dear Lillian who loves us all and wants only for us to be kind to each other."

Joanna smiled. "I agree with you completely."

Amanda blinked, reminding Joanna of a beautiful china doll she'd seen as a child in a toy store window, a china doll with eyes that could open and shut. "You do?"

"Sure. It'll be the best thing for everybody if we can just let bygones be bygones." The words weren't hard for Joanna to say because she meant them, though she knew both Burnett and Amanda well enough to doubt that it would all be smooth sailing.

Joanna was an optimist at heart. She chose to believe that someday the Clinton brothers would work out their differences and she and Amanda would become, if not friends, at least cordial acquaintances.

"Well, I'm just wonderfully relieved," Amanda was saying. "And now, I think we need to put our heads together about the party."

Joanna took another bracing sip of coffee. "The what?"

"Joey," Amanda clucked her tongue in a patronizing way that was supremely irritating. "I realize you get terribly absorbed in those little paintings of yours, but you do have other responsibilities now. Mike's birthday. It's August second, a little over a week away. I thought we could resurrect the old family tradition and give him a party at the original Chilly Lilly's."

Joanna smiled to herself. Way back when, they'd had some great times at Lillian's first ice-cream shop. In her mind's eye, she could see them all as children, wearing party hats and scooping syrupy sundaes into their eager mouths. Once Casey had used his spoon as a slingshot, and started an ice-cream fight. By the time Burnett stopped it, there was mocha fudge dripping from the old-fashioned milk glass light fixture overhead and nuts and maraschino cherries in everyone's hair.

In the free-association way that her artist's mind worked, Joanna recalled the dream she'd had on the night she and Casey had decided to marry, the dream of the adult Casey at the ice-cream shop. That might be interesting, she thought. Two paintings: one of the ice-cream fight long ago, and one of the adult Casey standing in the archway of the storeroom in a sort of dreamlike Chilly Lilly's, with hazy green walls moving up into nothingness....

"Joey, have you heard a word I've said?" Amanda's exasperated complaint brought her back to the here and now.

"Sorry, just thinking. I think a party would be a great idea. Now when did you say you wanted to have it?"

"Mike's birthday. Wednesday, the second. It's rather short notice, but I'm sure if we start calling today, we can get a few of his little friends to agree to come."

Joanna remembered her meeting with the bank representative. "Fine. But can we make it the following Saturday? We're going out of town for a few days. I have some appointments in Los Angeles."

"You're dragging Mike down there on his *birthday?*" Amanda made it sound as if Joanna had just invented a new form of child abuse.

"Come on, Amanda. Mike loves to go places. And he'll still get his party, if we have it when we return."

"Joey, you are going to need to get your priorities in order, if you hope to make this absurd marriage of yours work."

Joanna took a slow, deep breath and replied quietly. "My priorities are in order, Amanda. Now, shall we set the date of the party for the fifth?"

"I suppose I'll have to do it all myself, since you're going to be so busy."

That was the final straw. "Tell you what, Amanda. Forget the party, all right? Casey and I will take Mike to Magic Mountain while we're in Southern California."

Realizing she'd pushed it too far, Amanda turned contrite. "Oh, no please. I was being silly. Of course I'd love to do it." For all her poise and prettiness, Amanda suddenly looked very lost. Joanna found herself feeling sorry for her, and wondering about the deep-rooted dissatisfaction Amanda must feel in her life to be so relentlessly looking for opportunities to aggravate an already difficult situation.

Families, Joanna thought wryly, remembering the words of one of her more eccentric artist-friends in Los Angeles.

Families give you the chance to get to know a lot of people with whom you would otherwise have nothing to do, her friend had said. In the case of Amanda Clinton, how right he was.

"Please, Joey," Amanda added. "I *want* to do it. I want to be involved."

Though her wiser self warned against it, Joanna couldn't say no to such a heartfelt plea. "All right."

Amanda smiled, looking relieved and almost grateful. "Oh, good. Now, I thought we could make it a surprise. I have a list that Lillian gave me of several of his friends. I'll call them right away. And I thought we could just let Chilly Lilly's give the party, since they do it so often for customers. They'll provide the favors and game suggestions and all that. Really, all we need to do is be there a little early to check things over. And

I can do that, so you can bring Mike after everybody else is there."

Joanna had been mentally rearranging her schedule, trying to squeeze in some time for hunting down party hats and noisemakers. But the arrangements were obviously going to be quite simple, contrary to what Amanda had tried to make Joanna think at first. "That'll be fine," Joanna said.

Amanda pulled a leather appointment book from her bag and hastily jotted in it. "Wonderful. So that's Saturday the fifth at . . . two?"

"Fine."

"Well, then." Amanda put the appointment book back into her bag, and stood up. "I should be going, my meeting's at 9:30." Joanna started to get to her feet. "No, don't get up. I'll just go through the gate." Amanda smiled angelically. "Oh, Joey. I'm so glad we had this talk."

Joanna smiled back at her and murmured a low assent, not quite able to bring herself to say me too, since the "talk" hadn't really solved anything.

"I'm sorry I had to barge in on you without warning, but when I see that something needs to be confronted, I just do it, you understand?"

"Completely."

"And I want you to know I regret that little scene we had at your wedding, though I still feel you had no right to—"

"Amanda, I thought we were going to let bygones be bygones?"

"Oh, yes. Of course, you're right. Saturday the fifth, then. At two o'clock?"

"Sounds good."

Her slim back charm-school straight, Amanda glided toward the gate to the front yard.

Joanna remained in her seat, staring at the mosaic tile that rimmed the pool. She was trying to tell herself that things would be better between herself and Amanda from now on, and yet she could not really bring herself to believe it.

Lost in thought, she didn't sense Casey standing behind her until he put his hands on her shoulders. She jumped a little, and then grinned up at him.

"Is the dragon lady still breathing fire at her innocent in-laws?" he asked, half-teasingly. He began to knead the tired muscles in her upper back.

Joanna closed her eyes and let her head fall forward. "I can handle her." She sighed. "A little to the left. That's good. If you ever get tired of running Clinton Airfield, you could become a masseur."

"What's she up to now?"

"She wants us all to get along."

"That's refreshing, even if it's not very believable."

"And we're giving Mike a surprise party at Chilly Lilly's on the fifth, after we get back from Los Angeles."

"After *we* get back?" His fingers felt wonderful, working their soothing magic. His voice sounded pleased. "Does that mean you want us to go with you?"

She opened her eyes to slits and lifted her head a bit, so she could see his face above hers. "Sure, I do. Didn't we agree on that yesterday?" An uncertain look crossed his face, and then disappeared. It happened so fast, Joanna wasn't even sure she'd seen it. It surprised her because Casey so rarely looked uncertain. "I want you to come," she said levelly.

"I thought maybe you'd be ready for a break from us by now. Especially after a prebreakfast visit from the original wicked sister-in-law."

She took one of the hands that massaged her shoulder and interlaced her fingers with his. "A break from Amanda, definitely. But from you and Mike. Never." She pulled him around so they faced each other. "Is there something you're not telling me?"

"About what?"

"I don't know, lately..."

"Yes?"

She looked at him. Here they were again, two people who'd always had plenty to say to each other in the midst of another dangling conversation.

"Something's happened between us," she said bravely.

"Joey, it'll all work out," he said.

Joanna could tell by the tone of his voice that he didn't want to pursue the subject, and she didn't know quite how to approach it herself. There was the sex issue. It suddenly occurred to her she might bring it up in an oblique fashion by mentioning birth control.

Dragging in a breath, she managed to say, "I thought I'd get a doctor's appointment this week. Maybe go back on the Pill." The second of two serious relationships she'd shared had ended over a year before, and Joanna hadn't needed to worry about protecting herself from pregnancy since. A nervous laugh escaped her. "Everything's been so crazy. We hardly had time to think about preventing surprises."

Not that we've needed to so far, she added grimly to herself.

"Right," he said. He was looking at her in that unfathomable way he'd developed recently. "Good idea."

"I should, then," she heard herself continuing inanely, "go back on the Pill?"

"It always worked fine for you, didn't it?" he asked back.

"Yes, fine."

"Then, fine. Do it."

Casey, of course, knew all about her past close relationships with men. By the same token, he'd come to her to help him understand when a long-term relationship of his own had ended badly; his lover, Annie Devon, had accused him of being incapable of making a real commitment.

He'd ended up admitting to Joanna then that Annie had probably been right.

"Sometimes I think I'll never really fall in love in any lasting sense," Casey had confessed. "That it's just not in me. The idea of a lifetime commitment scares me to death. It makes me feel trapped, as if my big brother might finally win out and there I'll be, nose to the grindstone, grounded with a backbreaking load of responsibilities for the rest of my life."

He'd gone on to say that he knew in his mind that a deep relationship with a woman didn't have to be that way, but convincing his feelings of that was another matter altogether.

Joanna had teased him to lighten his mood. "Some smart girl will set her sights on you and not give up. She'll run you to ground. Eventually."

Never in the world would she have imagined then that he'd end up committed to Joanna herself.

Was that the root of the painful awkwardness between them now? Now that he was in the marriage, did he feel horribly trapped?

She'd asked him on their wedding night if he regretted what they'd done. He'd said no. If she kept harping at him about it, then he'd decide for sure that he'd made a giant mistake.

He was still standing in front of her, still wearing that inscrutable expression. She said, her voice hesitant, “Casey, I just feel like something's bothering you.”

“Everything's fine,” he said.

“You're sure?”

“Positive.”

Joanna gave up. She said, sounding lame, “Well, great. Then as far as Los Angeles goes, we'll fly down together, the three of us, on Monday the thirty-first. We'll come back up on Friday in time for the party on Saturday.”

“Fine,” Casey said. “We can take the Citation.” He mentioned his Cessna six-seater of which he was justifiably proud. “It'll be fun.”

“Yes, fun,” she said, and forced a smile.

Chapter Seven

Mike was cranky on the afternoon flight down to Los Angeles a week later, but Joanna hardly noticed. She was too keyed up over the coming interview with the Desert Empire Savings representative, and her meeting with Althea at the gallery after that.

They flew into Burbank Airport, then took an unpleasant cab ride to West Hollywood. The summer day was hot—in the high nineties. The air conditioning in the cab didn't work, and neither did the rear windows, so the three of them sat and sweltered.

When Joanna pushed open the door and confronted the long hall that ran the length of her upstairs apartment, a wave of air even hotter than that outside hit her in the face. Then she was aware of the smell of dust and paint solvents. For a moment, she stood there, perspiring in her light summer dress, peering over the threshold at what once had been her home. She wasn't giving up the flat; it was rent-controlled and ideal for her use whenever she needed to come to Los Angeles. But still it struck her, suddenly, that she really didn't live here anymore.

Behind her, Mike whined. "Do we have to stand here all day, Uncle Case? I'm hot."

Joanna turned to see Casey scooping the boy up in his arms. "Keep your shirt on, kid," Casey said. "We're getting there."

Mike leaned his head on Casey's shoulder. "My throat hurts," he mumbled. Then he sneezed.

Casey and Joanna exchanged a look over the boy's red-blond head. Then Joanna reached out and felt his forehead.

"He's warmer than he should be, even given that it's a hot day," she said. "I've got a thermometer in the medicine cabinet."

She led the way into the apartment, down the long hall to the extra bedroom, where Casey gently lowered Mike onto the bed and then returned to the door to bring in their suitcases. Joanna found the thermometer, stuck it in Mike's mouth and admonished him to keep it firmly under his tongue for four full minutes. She instructed him to watch the second hand on the clock by the bed. Then, while the boy stared intently at the clock and Casey went to the kitchen to get some cold drinks, Joanna started up the window air conditioners in both the bedrooms and in the studio-living room.

Mike's temperature was just over a hundred, so they tucked him into the bed and Casey made a quick trip to the corner store to buy throat lozenges and children's aspirin.

By dark, Mike was suffering from a full-blown case of the flu. He was feverish and coughing and tyrannical to both his uncle and Joanna. He finally dropped off to sleep at about ten o'clock.

Joanna and Casey ordered a large pizza and ate it at the kitchen table to the hum of the air conditioner and the occasional screams of sirens out in the Los Angeles night.

"He'll be on the mend by morning," Casey assured her.

Joanna smiled at him in vague agreement. She knew Mike would be fine. Right then, she was thinking of how she needed to put two finished paintings of Emily and another of Mike in her van the next morning, so she could show them to Althea after the meeting with the bank representative. The idea for the show at the gallery must be presented just so, to capture Althea's interest. The style of this show would lean toward photo-realism, and Althea's tastes ran to the more abstract.

"Anybody home in there?" she heard Casey teasing.

"Oh," Joanna laughed, embarrassed. "Sorry. Just thinking."

"Nervous about tomorrow?" he asked.

"A little."

"You'll be terrific," he told her. "And you should get to bed early, to be fresh."

She looked at him over the remains of their pizza. He had his chin on his fist, his elbow braced on the table. His strong neck looked very tanned where it disappeared into the collar of his blue sport shirt. "Yes," she said. "Early."

At that moment, Joanna discovered she was no longer thinking about her meetings the next day. Instead, her mind had conjured up an image of the way the man beside her had looked, asleep beneath the sheet the morning after their wedding. And then she found herself remembering the feel of his hand caressing her breast when he'd kissed her the night before that.

They'd been married a week and a half, and still they kept to their separate beds at either end of the landing in the house in Sacramento. Here in Los Angeles, she couldn't help thinking, Mike had the spare room. There was a Japanese futon bed in the studio/living room, but wouldn't it be much more natural for her and Casey to just share the bed in her room?

She silently admitted to herself that every day since their hasty wedding she'd become more and more aware of her best friend as a man. The truth was that she had come to desire him, and she longed for him to share the sweet yearning that grew stronger day by day.

I want him, Joanna thought, marveling, really want him—and I'm scared to death he's never going to want me back....

Bewilderingly, she recalled a conversation she'd shared with Michelle Bennet, Casey's first steady girlfriend back in high school. They had been in the girl's rest room, where Michelle spent a lot of time touching up her makeup during breaks between classes. Joanna had purposely sought Michelle out, because she wanted to be on good terms with anyone who was important to her best friend.

"Casey says you two are just friends." Michelle, who was pretty in a tough sort of way, had been piling more mascara onto her already impressive black eyelashes. Her inky eyes slid to Joanna's in the big mirror over the sinks.

"That's right," Joanna had replied.

Michelle lowered her voice to a whisper. "Come on. You mean you never even fooled around a little?"

"Nope," Joanna had said. "We've been friends forever." Precisely six years, at that time, but to the teenage Joanna, it had seemed like eternity. "We just don't think of each other that way."

"Weird," Michelle had decided after a moment.

Joanna had felt defensive. "What we have is special. Why ruin it with sex?"

"Hey," Michelle had retorted. "Do you see me arguing? You just keep what you got with him—and I'll take the rest." She'd leaned toward Joanna, so their images in the mirror were almost touching. And she'd whispered, her black eyes full of a feminine knowledge which Joanna had not possessed at the time. "I ain't complaining, Joey. Even though you're not interested, he's really great that way."

He's really great that way... Black-eyed Michelle's words echoed in her mind.

Joanna couldn't help but wonder: was he? And would she ever find out?

Joanna's face suddenly felt very warm. Beside her, Casey sat unmoving. He was watching her, his light eyes focused on the hollow of her throat, where she could feel the throb of her heightened pulse. And then his gaze traveled up, slowly, to her haphazardly pinned up hair that always became thicker and more unmanageable in the heat. Now, she had it anchored on her head with a huge plastic clip.

In a gesture that stunned her with its simple intimacy, Casey reached out and pinched the clip, removing it from her cloud of hair, which promptly fell full and wild around her face.

"Pretty," he said. "Thick and loose like that." He set the clip aside and lightly, in subtle strokes, combed her hair with his fingers, from her temples out to the wild-curling ends.

Joanna swallowed. It was almost as if he had read her mind. As if he knew what she wanted of him, and had simply decided to give it to her.

"What—" she had to swallow again "—what are you doing, Casey?"

"Touching," he said. "Is that all right?"

Joanna didn't trust herself to speak, so she nodded.

"I'm glad." He went on combing her hair with his fingers.

Lately, she didn't understand him at all. She knew him better than any other human being on earth. He was her best friend. Yet he'd left her alone on their wedding night and had barely touched her since. And now he was looking at her like... he was touching her like...

Joanna's thought faded off into a chaos of pure sensation as, holding her gaze captive, he laid two fingers against the throbbing pulse in the hollow of her throat. The absolute familiarity of the gesture took her breath away. Somehow, he *knew* she'd been aware of that pulse, of its quickening. And he touched it as if to share her excitement with her. Her breathing deepened, and she was suddenly conscious of her breasts rising and falling beneath the light cotton of her dress, of her nipples, hardening though he had not even touched them.

His fingers lay quiescent against her throat for seconds without end, as if he were absorbing her sensations, taking them inside himself, and then, through the fingertips that had received those sensations, passing them back to her, redoubled.

"What is happening, Casey?" she heard herself ask.

"Shall I stop?" he asked by way of reply. His fingers left the secret pulse in her throat to travel downward.

Joanna couldn't speak period.

With the flat of his palm, he very lightly rubbed her left breast where it strained erect beneath her loose cotton dress.

"Tell me to stop, Joey," he said. "If that's what you want, I'll understand." His voice had grown serious in its huskiness. He went on teasing her breast with his palm.

"Don't stop," she heard herself sigh, letting her head drop back as she strained her breasts toward him. He obliged her body's request by stroking the other breast.

Then he pulled his hand away. Joanna gave a tiny cry of loss and lifted her head.

He smiled at her, slowly, and nodded toward the window.

It took her a moment to understand. Making love in front of the window wasn't as private as he wanted it to be.

"In the bedroom?" she asked.

He stood up and took her hand. They stopped briefly at the room where Mike slept and Joanna went in to feel his forehead and straighten the covers. Mike's breathing rattled a little from the congestion in his chest.

"His forehead is still warm," Joanna said. "But I think he's okay."

They went on to her room with its buff-colored walls and accents of the cool, soothing green found in the deepest part of a forest.

Casey sat on the edge of her bed and pulled his sport shirt over his head, tossing it on the fat green velvet chair in the corner.

Joanna hovered by the door, watching him, feeling suddenly as if she were moving in a dream. Casey was hunching over to remove his shoes when he stopped, without warning, and looked at her. He sat upright, one shoe off and one shoe on.

He said, "Have you changed your mind?"

She said, "No. I was just wondering, I guess—why now?"

He said, "I thought, the way you looked at me in the kitchen, that you were ready."

The dreamlike quality of the moment made her bold. She said, "I was ready on our wedding night."

He shrugged. "If you say so." He bent just long enough to slide off the other shoe and get rid of his socks. Then he stood up and approached her. He came within inches of her, and she could feel the radiant heat of his body reaching out to hers.

"But forget then. We can't change then. The question is, do you want me now, Joey?" he said.

"Yes." Her voice was firm and steady.

He stroked her bare arm, in an up-and-down movement. It caused little shivers to run over her skin. Then he slid both of his hands to her hips and, very slowly, he began to gather up the skirt of her dress.

The slow bunching and raising of her skirt was one of the most erotic sensations she'd ever experienced. It shocked her as much as aroused her that it should turn out to be Casey who would make her body vibrate with such overwhelming sensuality. In her previous intimate relationships, she'd enjoyed sex, but not like this, never so totally—and so far, Casey had done no more than touch her breast and slowly—oh, so slowly—raise her skirt.

The cool air from the window air conditioner caressed her legs as he uncovered them. Soon, the skirt was bunched in his fists at her waist.

He pulled her against his chest. And then he kissed her, lingeringly, his mouth teasing at first, and then closing possessively over hers. Joanna gave herself over to his mouth, as his hands rode her hips, rubbing her bunched skirt against the tender skin of her pelvis.

Then he pulled back. Joanna swayed unsteadily toward him, as if, during the lingering kiss, her body had become magnetized to his.

"Open your eyes, Joey," he said.

She did, slowly, and found herself looking into his.

He continued, his eyes holding hers. "I want to see your eyes while I look at you. All of you."

He pulled the loose dress up and over her head. She stood before him, her gaze locked with his. She was wearing only her sandals, her bikini panties and her bra.

He put his hands back on her hips, the warm touch sending a bolt of sensory lightning straight to the secret place between her thighs. Then he turned her around and guided her backward, until she was sitting on the end of the bed.

He knelt, and slipped her sandals off, one at a time. Feeling weak-limbed, she leaned back on her hands and looked at the strong muscles in his shoulders and arms, at his bent head, as he held her foot in his hands.

There was something so trusting in the way he revealed the back of his neck to her, something so honest and vulnerable. Within the heat and hunger he'd aroused in her body, her heart melted, too.

It seemed as though she had always known him. They had shared the need to find different lives than the ones their families had laid out for them. Casey had longed to fly; Joanna had wanted only to paint pictures that would capture the beauty and mystery of all creation. Always, they'd encouraged and nurtured each other's dreams.

But now, to see this other side of him. To see him as a man, offering her his bent head, the vulnerable back of his neck. To see the totality of him, her friend since childhood, was beautiful and terrifying and almost more than she could bear.

"Casey..." She breathed his name.

He raised his head. His eyes were full of heat and knowing. He said nothing. He didn't have to. He placed his hands, open, on either side of her ankles, clasping them. And then he slid his hands, slowly, up the sides of her calves, over her knees to her thighs, leaving a trail of sensual heat behind, so that the skin of her legs burned with his knowing of them. His eyes, meanwhile, held hers captive, daring her, as they'd so often done, but in a new way.

Daring her to see him, all of him, and to utterly surrender to what was happening between them now.

He slipped his middle fingers up over her hips, eliciting a gasp from her which made him smile.

He hooked her panties with his fingers and gave a gentle tug. Joanna lifted her hips so he could slide them off.

He took her bra next, in a leisurely fashion, enticing her first by massaging the curve of her waist, and by insinuating his fingers beneath her bra strap and lightly stroking the skin there with the back of his hand.

At last, as her eyes pleaded with his, he unhooked the front clasp and slid it over her arms and away. Her breasts, the dusky nipples already achingly hard, were revealed to him.

Did he call her beautiful? If not, he made her feel that way, as he moved up between her legs to make slow tender love to her breasts, both with his hands and his hungry, seeking mouth.

By then, Joanna had thrown her head back, too transported to maintain the heady contact with his eyes. But he allowed that, taking satisfaction, she perceived, in the way her body gave over completely to the magic in his touch and the tender urgings that came from his lips.

Gently, he pulled back again. And his hand strayed to the liquid center of her. He loved her there, with his touch, as she opened herself utterly to him. In that way, he brought her to shuddering satisfaction, until she fell back against the comforter, spent.

For endless moments, she lost the touch of his skin against hers. She bore the loss well at first, still pulsing with sweet afterglow. But then she missed him.

"Casey?" She lifted her heavy head from the pillow to see him just stepping out of his briefs at the foot of the bed.

"I'm here, Joey."

She looked at him. And she thought he was the handsomest, most perfectly formed man she had ever seen. He was fully aroused, and seeing that, she felt desire build in her again.

She held out her arms. Casey moved into them. The magical sensual dance of pleasure began again.

Joanna said his name over and over, as she revelled in the feel of his body against her, the teasing scrape of wiry chest hair against her tender breasts, in the hardness of his thighs against hers, and the sparring play of their tongues as their lips met and joined.

She touched him. And he astonished her again by giving himself up to her pleasuring hands just as moments before she had given herself to his. He let her bring him to completion like that, without even entering her. Joanna thought that marvelous, that he was willing, in lovemaking, to surrender as totally as he wanted her to. After that, they rested, his head against the soft curve of her neck.

They talked for a time about nothing of consequence, like new lovers sometimes do, more for the sound and play of voice to voice in the aftermath of passion than for any of the things that might have needed to be said.

Joanna left him, briefly, to turn off the air conditioners and open the windows, letting in the warm night air. Casey watched her, as she returned to him where he waited on the bed.

She saw that desire was moving again, a slow heat in his eyes. Casey reached for her, brought her down to him and found her instantly ready for the total joining he sought.

He reared up over her, and came into her. Joanna opened for him like a flower for the sun, astounded by the wonder of it, marveling at herself and Casey, woman and man, after all these years.

They found fulfillment together that time, and as the waves of pleasure vibrated between their loved bodies, Joanna cried aloud with the beauty and the wonder and the joy of what he made her feel.

Afterward, unspeaking, he held her close for a time. Then they peeled back the covers of the bed and tucked themselves beneath the sheet.

As she drifted toward slumber wrapped in Casey's arms, Joanna felt certain, for the first time since their impetuous marriage, that everything would work out. Even if Casey feared being trapped in marriage, he was capable of desiring her. Beyond the emotional and mental affinities they shared, beyond their commitment to Mike's well-being, they could now count on the bond of physical pleasure as well.

* * *

The next morning, Mike was still feverish and fussy. Joanna coaxed him to drink some juice and read to him for a while, before Casey shooed her out of the bedroom to get ready for her lunch date.

After carting the canvasses down to her van, Joanna took a leisurely bath and dressed with care in a trim ice-pink gabardine dress.

Joanna met with Niki Tori, the interior designer from Desert Empire Savings, at an upscale California-cuisine restaurant in Century City at 12:30. Two hours later, she shook hands with Niki—they were on a first-name basis by then—and floated out into Century Plaza on cloud nine.

The specific figures would be worked out between Niki and Althea, who often acted as Joanna's agent, but the commission was definitely *on*. The time frame, which had been Joanna's main concern, was wonderfully broad. Niki didn't need the six massive acrylic texture studies or the series of smaller signed prints until the first of next year. Except for signing the contracts, Joanna could put the commission from her mind until she'd finished the collection of paintings for her show at the gallery.

The meeting with Althea at three o'clock was also a success, though there were one or two rocky moments. It took some convincing to make Althea warm to Joanna's idea.

"If I wanted Norman Rockwell, I'd go looking for back copies of the *Saturday Evening Post*," the gallery owner had remarked snidely.

But Joanna had brought out her charcoal sketches as well as the finished portraits of Emily and Mike.

Althea found the two studies of Emily, sitting in a bentwood chair in front of a black drop curtain, haunting. And she noted that, in the painting of Mike, Joanna had managed to capture that engaging combination of enthusiasm and solemnity that made the boy unique.

Soon enough, Joanna and Althea were poring over the charcoal sketches together and Althea was outlining her own ideas for how the show would be hung, explaining with conspicuous excitement how she'd move the tall display screens around to show each canvas to best advantage.

Joanna left the gallery at five, flushed with excitement and exhilaration. She couldn't wait to tell Casey all about it.

Though traffic was the usual Los Angeles rush hour nightmare, the San Vicente address of the gallery was less than two miles away from her apartment. Within fifteen minutes of waving goodbye to Althea, Joanna pulled into her parking space behind her apartment building.

Since she'd left the paintings with Althea, she only needed to tuck her sketch pad under her arm and race for the stairs, her joy at her success bubbling over into a happy laugh.

She took the steps to her door two at a time, in spite of the heat and the difficulty of such acrobatics in her elegant high-heeled shoes. She burst into the air-conditioned coolness of the apartment calling Casey's name.

"In here!" His voice came from the bathroom.

Joanna hurried down the long hall past Mike's open door and the room she and Casey had shared for the first time the night before. The bathroom door, at the end of the hall, was open.

She entered to find Casey kneeling by the tub and a naked, drooping Mike inside.

"What's the matter? How is he?" she asked.

Casey looked up at her. His eyes were bleak and full of fear. "His temperature just shot up. I don't understand it. It's a hundred and six."

Chapter Eight

Joanna dropped her purse and sketchbook on the counter behind her and knelt beside Casey at the tub. Using a big plastic cup from the kitchen, he was ladling the bathwater over the little boy's bowed shoulders.

"I called his pediatrician in Sacramento. He said I had to get his fever down, to give him the children's pain reliever and to put him in a lukewarm bath."

"Too cold, don't like cold," Mike said in an odd little sing-song, shaking his head. He remained upright, but barely. He was staring blankly at the tub fixtures.

"How long's he been like this?" Joanna asked.

"I don't know for sure. I guess he was getting worse all day, though I didn't want to acknowledge it. He got cranky after you left, and then he seemed tired, so I let him sleep. I checked on him at two and three and he was feverish, but not too bad. Then I left him alone for a while. About half an hour ago, I went to check on him and he was burning up."

"When did you give him the pain reliever?"

"At least twenty minutes ago," Casey said. "Do you think we should get him to an emergency room?"

Joanna tested the water. "This is too warm," she said. "It's not going to lower his temperature any."

Casey kept tenderly pouring the water over Mike. "I had it a little colder before. He cried. It made him uncomfortable."

Joanna stuck her hand in the water and pulled the plug. Then she turned on the cold tap full blast. Mike jumped, and slid back away from the cold jet. "No, no, cold, cold..."

"What are you doing?" Casey roughly shoved her aside and shut off the tap. "I told you, he doesn't like that."

"It has to be colder, Casey."

"No." He put the plug back in and turned on the taps again, to the same warm temperature.

Joanna stared at him, just beginning to put together what was happening inside him. Right then, she realized, he was thinking only a little more clearly than Mike himself. Casey Clinton had tested fighter jets for the navy after finishing second in his class. To this day, there was nothing he enjoyed more than hanging by the prop of his Stearman Biplane for endless seconds before dropping gracefully into a tailslide.

He was the kind of pilot who, even to the last moment, would keep thinking calmly of what strategy to take next to pull himself out of a low-level stall.

But at that moment, he was so terrified for his nephew that he couldn't accept that he would have to let the boy cry from the cold if they wanted to get his temperature down.

"We need to get him to the hospital," Casey was saying. "Joey, get something to put on him..." He reached for a bath towel.

"No." Joanna grabbed his arm. "You go call the doctor again."

He shook her off, anger sparking in his eyes. "What do you mean, call the doctor?" He swore. "The doctor's in Sacramento. We need help here!"

"You go call the doctor now," she demanded in a no-nonsense voice. "You ask him what lukewarm means. You ask him if Mike's going to have to cry a little from the cold if his fever is going to be lowered."

"What the hell do you know?" Then, he stood up and glared down at her. "You never had a kid! I never had a kid! What the hell do people like us know about something like this?"

She looked at him, and she didn't allow her gaze to waver. "Call. Now."

Miraculously, he did. Like someone in a trance, he turned and left the room.

He returned in a few minutes wearing a sheepish expression.

"Okay, do it," he said.

Joanna pulled the plug and began the process of cooling the water. Mike scooted backward to the end of the tub, shaking his head.

Casey said, "He'll be screaming in a few minutes."

"But his fever will go down," Joanna reminded him. "From what I understand about kids and high fevers, they get them—and they can be serious. But the important thing is not to let them go on for too long. We'll get his fever down and then we'll call the doctor back to find out what we should do next."

Casey attempted a grin. "Since when did you learn all this about kids?"

"It's secondhand," she told him, and then elaborated in an effort to distract him from his distress over Mike. "Mostly from Aunt Edna. She did raise six kids, after all. And she always says she never could have done it if the little devils weren't so darn resilient. 'You give them love,' Aunt Edna always says, 'and they'll bounce back from anything.'"

"Cold, cold," Mike mumbled. He'd started to shiver.

Casey's attempt at a smile faded. He was still hovering near the door. "Maybe I should let you deal with this," he said.

Joanna considered this suggestion, while Mike's whimpering became more insistent.

True, the easiest course would be to tend to the nursing herself, since it upset Casey so much. But letting Casey off the hook in this painful duty would be the wrong approach. He was in for the duration when it came to raising Mike. And he needed to know that he could do whatever had to be done himself if the need arose.

Joanna said, "Are we in this together or not?"

Mike was shaking all over now, and he'd started to cry. "It's too cold!" he insisted, between sobs. "It's cold, cold, it's too cold!"

"God," Casey said. But he left the haven of the doorway and came to kneel beside her.

For the first time since Joanna had entered the bathroom, Mike's eyes cleared. He looked right at his uncle through a fat rain of tears. "Uncle Case, it's too cold! Turn it off, now!" He levered his small shaking body upright to grab the rim of the rub, and tried to climb out.

"You'll have to hold him down," Joanna said. "And I'll pour the water over his shoulders." Mike was halfway out of the tub. "Casey," Joanna said. "Please..." She reached toward Mike, to keep him in the tub, since Casey seemed to be frozen beside her.

But then Casey said quietly. "It's all right. I'll do it."

And he did. First, he took the boy's thin shoulders and gently but firmly pushed him back down in the cool water. Then he held him there, not relenting though at first Mike screamed and flailed his arms about.

As he held him, Casey spoke to Mike soothingly, until at last the child stopped fighting the pain of the cold water against his burning skin. In the end, Mike sat shivering and sobbing while Casey comforted him with soft words and Joanna ladled the cold water over his chest and shoulders.

Casey looked over at her, his mouth a grim line. "How long does this have to go on?"

Joanna had no idea, but she knew now was not the time to show Casey her ignorance. "I'd say we should give it a good fifteen minutes, at least. Give the water—and the pain reliever—a chance to really work."

"Terrific," Casey murmured, and then turned his attention back to Mike. "It's okay," he said. "Only a little while, kid, and you'll be feeling a lot better."

Joanna glanced at her watch to start timing, and then went back to pouring the water over the quivering child.

Somehow, the fifteen minutes passed, though Casey said later that it didn't seem like they ever would.

At last, Joanna said, "Okay. Take him out."

Casey scooped the shaking boy against his chest, while Joanna got a big towel to wrap around him.

Back in the spare room, they took his temperature. It was down four degrees to one hundred and two.

"Thank God," Casey breathed.

Joanna got him to drink some juice while Casey called the doctor again.

"He says to give him the pain reliever every four hours, and keep him drinking liquids," Casey reported. "If the fever goes back up, we call him right away. Otherwise, he gave me the name of a pediatrician in Van Nuys where we can take him tomorrow."

Mike's eyes were already drooping against his flushed cheeks. Tenderly, Joanna tucked the sheet around him and then she and Casey tiptoed from the room.

Casey went out for Chinese food as Joanna changed from her soaked dress to a pair of shorts and a tank top.

As the big orange sun disappeared behind the rooftops, they took turns checking on Mike, and coaxing liquids down his throat. By midnight both Joanna and Casey felt that the worst was behind them.

They sat on the futon in the living room/studio, and Casey asked her how her meetings had gone. She proudly reported her success and he congratulated her.

"It's been quite a day for you," he said, then, and pulled her head down to rest on his shoulder.

She snuggled against him, feeling bone-weary, but content. "It's been pretty challenging for you, too," she said.

He made a sound in his throat. "Clearly I have a lot to learn about giving Mike what he needs."

"You love him. You hated to see him suffer." In a reassuring manner, Joanna put her hand on his chest. Beneath his light knit skirt, she could feel the steady beating of his heart.

"I was an idiot." He kissed the crown of her head, his breath teasing her hair. "Seeing Mike so sick reminded me of Emily," he confessed. "Of being powerless, of having to sit by and watch someone you love suffering, and not knowing what the hell to do about it. I started thinking that maybe Burnett was right."

She reached up, by feel, and put two fingers on his lips. "Don't say it. Don't even *think* it, Casey Clinton."

He spoke against her fingers. "Thank God you came in when you did or heaven knows what would have—"

Joanna interrupted again. "What *did* happen was that we got his fever down. I'll bet you he'll be well enough for his party Saturday. Really. Like Aunt Edna says—"

He chuckled. "I know, I know. 'Give 'em love, and they bounce back from anything.' "

"You got it."

"The question is," Casey murmured with another rueful chuckle, "will *we* survive?"

"I think we're doing okay," Joanna said.

"That's easy to say now. We're four hundred miles away from Burnett and Amanda. Getting through a one-hundred-and-six-degree fever is nothing compared to dealing with my family on a day-to-day basis."

"Burnett and Amanda are not your whole family," Joanna told him. "Your sister was like a sister to *me*. And your mother is a dear friend."

"Right," he said, not sounding too convinced. She fidgeted a little, trying to get comfortable on the small couch/bed. "Come on," he told her. "Swing your legs up here."

Obediently, Joanna swung her bare legs across his thighs. He laid a warm hand on her knee. Joanna squirmed a little. Not from discomfort, but from the memory of the pleasure they'd shared the night before.

Their bodies, at least, were totally at ease with each other again—and in a more intimate, and infinitely more pleasurable way than they had been when they were just friends.

In fact, after what they'd faced together this evening, she felt closer to him, more relaxed emotionally, than she had since the night they'd decided to get married. Maybe now would be a good time to talk about the distance she'd been feeling from him lately.

"Casey?"

"Um?"

"Remember when you and Annie broke up three years ago?"

"Yeah."

"She accused you of being afraid of commitment."

"I remember," he said.

"You told me then that you thought she was right. That the idea of a lifetime commitment scared you to death."

"That was then," he said. His voice, she thought, was much too expressionless.

"Casey, we need to talk about it. There's nothing wrong with your feeling that way, really. I can understand completely, I really can. I mean, every day I wonder—"

"What?"

"Well, I wonder if we did the right thing. I feel it's a big step for both of us, and I pray we'll make it work."

"Do you want out?" he demanded. "Is that what you're saying?"

Somehow, in the space of a few short exchanges, the conversation had gotten completely away from her. All the easy, relaxed feeling had evaporated. The air crackled with tension.

Joanna was sitting up straight by then, and she tried to pull her legs off of his thighs. But he held onto them.

"Just tell me," he said. "Do you want out?"

"Casey, I'm just trying to get us to talk about what's going on here."

"Do you want out?"

"No, no," she found herself hastening to reassure him. "Casey, really. It's working out fine for me. Honestly."

"Good."

"But Casey..." Hesitantly, she touched his forehead, smoothing his hair back.

"What?"

"You seem guarded. You were never guarded with me before."

He shrugged in a casual way. But the look in his eyes wasn't casual at all. "I put you in a difficult position, that's all," he said. "I feel badly about that. But you know what?"

"What?"

"I don't feel badly enough about it to let you off the hook."

"I didn't ask to be let off the hook."

He grinned, and his gaze slid down to her bare legs stretched out across his own. "Then what are we arguing about?"

"Well, we're not. Or at least, that wasn't my intention."

"Good. Come here." He pulled her closer, until she was actually sitting on his lap.

His body felt so good against hers, that Joanna gave up her attempt to get him to tell her what was going on inside him. Ultimately, she told herself, their marriage was necessary if he wanted to keep Mike. They were getting along well together, all things considered. And if he wanted to keep his doubts and fears to himself, that was his business. She certainly wasn't going to nag him into confiding in her.

Casey nuzzled her neck. Joanna sighed and snuggled closer to him.

She decided to give it one more try. "Casey?" Her voice was husky with the beginnings of desire.

"Yeah?" He began kissing her ear.

"I would do my best to understand anything you wanted to tell me."

"I know, Joey," he murmured into the ear he was kissing. "You always have. And I do have something to tell you . . ."

"Yes?"

"I want to make love to you . . ."

"Casey Clinton," Joanna said. "That's not what I meant and you know it."

"Yeah, but do you *understand?*" His sexy whisper had a hint of laughter in it.

"Oh, I do understand," she told him, giving in to the sensual game he played so wonderfully. "Absolutely."

"Good."

Casey slowly ran his hand along her leg, lingering over the shape of her knee. Taking all the time in the world about it, his hand slid up her thigh to the hem of her shorts, where he teased her by slipping a finger under the hem and running it back and forth against her skin.

"Casey," she sighed.

"Want me to stop?"

"We should check on Mike."

"Right. I'll go." He set her neatly off his lap and stood up, oblivious of her small forlorn moan. He looked back at her, though, just before he reached the arch to the long hallway. "I could meet you in the bedroom in five minutes," he suggested. "It would save me another trip down this tunnel you call a hallway."

She gave him a naughty grin. "You don't want to try out my futon? It converts into a double bed." But then she thought of Mike. It was unlikely the boy would disturb them, but a locked door was the only way to be sure of that. "Oops. I forgot," she laughed. "We have a child."

He pretended to look regretful. "One of these days we'll have to come down here alone." He cast a speculative glance at her drawing board. "The erotic possibilities are endless."

"Casey, I'm shocked," she lied.

"You?" he scoffed. "Joey Vail, who dared me to take off all my clothes when we were twelve and dance naked in the vacant field four blocks from our houses?"

She hastened to correct him. "That wasn't about sex and you know it. That was a dare. No different than all the other times you dared me or I dared you."

He shook his head. "It *was* about sex," he said.

"What do you mean?"

"I mean I was damn thrilled you dared me to take off all my clothes with you. You played right into my most secret fantasies. I wanted to see you naked," he said. "I'd never seen a girl naked before, except Emily in the bathtub, and that didn't count. When I remember that dare, that's what I think of. Seeing you naked."

Joanna found she was blushing. "You never told me that before."

"You never asked." He grinned. "You were awful skinny," he added, "back when we were twelve."

"Why, you . . ." She picked up a small throw pillow and aimed it at his head.

"I was relieved last night," he went on blithely, "to see how much you've filled out." He ducked into the hallway just before the throw pillow connected with his head.

"Five minutes. The bedroom," he called back to her, though she couldn't see him.

"You were no Adonis yourself back then!" she called to him. She heard a distant chuckle in response.

Then she pulled herself to her feet, went to the kitchen to put the Chinese food cartons in the refrigerator and followed Casey down the long hallway.

When he joined her, he told her Mike was sleeping peacefully, and then he took her in his arms. They made love slowly at first, touching and teasing and getting to know each other's bodies all over again.

But as their desire escalated, their loving took on a frantic, hungry edge. Joanna reveled in it, in all the moods and tempos their lovemaking took. In the end, she clung to him, crying out his name, as he gave her her satisfaction and took his at the same time.

They lay together afterward, their moist bodies clinging together, and Joanna remembered the two of them, as they had been all those years ago, a pair of skinny children dancing naked underneath a spring sky.

Very gently, Casey pulled away. Joanna gave him a small moan in protest.

"Go to sleep," he told her. "I'll take the big chair in Mike's room, just to keep an eye on him."

Casey kissed her and pulled the sheet over her.

"You're a wonderful uncle," she murmured.

She felt his smile against her cheek as he kissed her once more. "'Night, Joey." And he was gone.

Before she surrendered to sleep, she experienced that sense of unease again. The night before she had told herself that their physical union was a good thing. And it was. But tonight, she couldn't help suspecting that Casey had used the new excitement between them to avoid opening up about his fears and doubts.

Chapter Nine

The next day, Wednesday, was Mike's birthday. Casey and Joanna sang a chorus of "Happy Birthday to You," while they took his morning temperature. Then they clapped wildly when the thermometer came out reading 98.6.

The pediatrician pronounced Mike successfully on the mend and declared that he should be ready to fly home by Friday as planned. Joanna bought a cake at the supermarket and produced a few gifts that she'd wrapped and put in her suitcase before the trip down. She also brought along presents from his paternal grandparents that had arrived from the Midwest the week before. Packages to open made the day special, and also served to keep Saturday's party the surprise it was intended to be.

Still weak from his bout with fever, Mike went to sleep before eight. And Casey and Joanna made slow, leisurely love in her forest-green bedroom.

Thursday, they remained in Los Angeles and Mike recuperated further. Early Friday they flew home.

In Sacramento, they took Mike to his own doctor, who advised an over-the-counter expectorant to get rid of the boy's lingering nighttime cough. During a moment when Mike was out of earshot, Joanna asked the doctor about the party the next day; the doctor said it should be fine as long as Mike went easy on the sweets and didn't overdo.

Saturday dawned a scorcher. It was well over eighty-five degrees by the pool when Joanna took a morning swim at nine o'clock to clear out the cobwebs from working late into the night. Casey returned at nine-thirty from the airfield where he'd gone to find out how Rhonda had managed in his absence. He and Mike both joined her in the pool. They played a rousing family game of Keep Away, with Joanna and Mike against Casey, who continually managed to leap from the water and snare the ball no matter what the other two did.

At noon, while they ate tuna sandwiches, Casey casually suggested that the three of them could drive over to Chilly Lilly's in an hour or two for ice cream.

"Is that where I'm having my party?" Mike asked.

Casey and Joanna looked at each other; somehow, Mike had figured it out. Casey cleared his throat, and Joanna knew he was about to ask, How did you know? Joanna shot him a pleading look. The agreement with Amanda was that the party would be a surprise; Joanna wanted to keep to the agreement, for the sake of improved family relations. She wanted to give Amanda no excuse, however thin, to stir up hostilities again.

"What makes you think you're having a party?" Joanna asked, her voice studiously noncommittal.

The six-year-old looked smug. "Uncle Burnett and Grandma Lilly didn't give me my presents yet, even though we've been home for a whole day." Mike swiped his nose with the back of his hand. Joanna frowned and handed him a tissue. "Oops, sorry," he said, taking the tissue and wiping his nose properly.

Mike passed back the used tissue. "So I'm right, huh?"

"Do you want to get ice cream or not?" Joanna asked.

"I get it," Mike said. "I'm supposed to pretend I'm surprised. Right?"

"Drink your milk," Joanna said, as Casey tried to keep from laughing.

Mike did his six-year-old best to act surprised when his friends jumped out at him from behind the ice-cream freezers. But he was too much a stranger to deception to make the behavior convincing.

"Wow, dinosaurs!" he said, commenting on the decorations after the squealing and greetings had died down. "I didn't expect dinosaur decorations. This is very excellent."

Over the boy's head, Amanda shot Joanna a chilly look for presumably having ruined her surprise. "I knew you'd like them Mike, so I picked them out especially," she said. "Now, how about a little game of pin the tail on Tyrannosaurus Rex."

"Wow, excellent," the boy said, and the game commenced.

Amanda had a number of entertainments lined up, and she conducted each of them with the skill of a social director. The children all received dinosaur activity books, and then connected the dots to make a Pterodactyl, the child who accomplished the task first winning the prize. They played Drop the Dinosaur in the Bottle, for which Amanda had provided an astonishing number of small, plastic Stegosauri.

In fact, as the party progressed, Joanna realized that Amanda had put a great deal of time and energy into this event. The number and variety of decorations and favors was way beyond anything Chilly Lilly's could ordinarily provide; when they had spoken of the party the previous week, Amanda had clearly stated she'd let the ice-cream shop furnish everything.

After feeling somewhat deceived at first, Joanna looked at Amanda's actions from a different perspective. She decided to be grateful that Mike's aunt was willing to do so much to give him the best party imaginable.

It was a little more difficult, however, to rationalize Amanda's cunningly treacherous behavior as the party progressed.

Subtly, in a hundred little ways, Amanda slighted Joanna. At one point she asked Lillian to help her jot down the children's names to put in a hat. She asked Casey and Burnett to move chairs and tables around to clear the floor for another game. She never invited Joanna to be involved in any way; but twice she asked Joanna to please get out of the way.

Joanna decided to be philosophical. She had known that it was unlikely that she and Amanda would ever be close. Furthermore, Joanna saw no reason at all to compete with her sister-in-law for Mike's affection; that would be extremely destructive. She reminded herself that Amanda *was* the hostess and told herself to be grateful that Mike was having such a terrific time.

More than once, she intercepted chagrined glances from Lillian, who saw all too well what was going on. Joanna smiled reassuringly at her mother-in-law, trying to telegraph the message with her eyes that she was bearing up. Once or twice, Joanna thought she caught a self-satisfied gleam in Burnett's dark eyes; it occurred to her that he was very pleased with the efficient way his wife had pushed Joanna to the sidelines. Joanna determinedly told herself that she simply couldn't afford to react to Burnett's smug, exasperating behavior.

One thing Joanna had learned from years of battling her parents when she was an intense, dissatisfied teenager was that it took at least two family members at odds with each other to make a family fight. If she didn't let Burnett or his wife get to her, then no family battle would ensue.

Joanna was quite pleased with her mature approach—until she happened to glance at Casey.

He was sitting backward in a straight chair at the long table where everyone had gathered to sing the birthday song. He was staring, calmly, at Amanda at the other end as Amanda helped Mike cut the Brontosaurus-shaped ice-cream cake. He looked utterly and completely relaxed. He seemed to feel Joanna's eyes on him and left off staring at his sister-in-law to acknowledge Joanna's glance.

He smiled at Joanna. The smile was ice-cold.

Joanna realized he was furious.

"Mike, honey, please," Amanda was saying in a coyingly affectionate voice. "Use a tissue when you wipe your nose." She whipped one out of her sleeve and handed it to Mike who obediently made use of it. "There," Amanda said, and then felt his forehead. "Well, at least it doesn't feel as if you're feverish." The day before, Joanna had spoken briefly over the phone with Amanda and had told her about Mike's illness in Los Angeles. It had seemed wiser to mention it herself than to have Amanda find out secondhand; no doubt Amanda would then accuse her of manufacturing a plot to keep family information from her.

Mike pushed Amanda's coddling hands away. "I'm fine, Aunt Amanda. Really. Now let me cut my cake."

"I'm glad," Amanda said. "It wouldn't do if Joanna had brought you out when you were still sick."

Casey stood up. "Amanda," he said. "I wonder if I could have a word with you, in private."

"Casey..." Joanna began, falling silent when he shot her a sharp look.

Burnett growled. "Now, just a minute here—"

Lillian, as usual, only smiled sheepishly.

Casey winked broadly at Burnett. "We'll be back in a flash, Big Brother." He was already at Amanda's side, taking her arm, and guiding her toward the storerooms in the back. "This is just something that can't wait another minute. Joey, help Mike cut the cake, would you?"

"Casey, I—" Joanna began.

"Do it," Casey cut her off, his tone pleasantly neutral for all the command in the words.

Amanda was too nonplussed by her brother-in-law's audacity to do anything but stare in astonishment. Then, she was dragged out of sight into the other room. For a moment, Joanna thought Burnett would follow, but then Lillian completely surprised her by placing a hand on his arm.

"Let it be, dear," she said pleasantly.

Burnett stayed where he was.

The children had already tuned out whatever boring adult things were going on among the grown-ups. One of the little boys had stolen one of the girl's Triceratops erasers and the girl began wailing. Mike was busy sawing the head off his ice-cream Brontosaurus.

"Yum, gumdrop eyeballs," he murmured, popping the eyeball in question into his mouth. Joanna reminded herself that the doctor had told her Mike was no longer contagious, so none of the other children were in danger of picking up his flu. Still, after reclaiming the wailing girl's eraser, she promptly took over the cake-cutting duties.

In a few minutes, Amanda and Casey rejoined the group. Joanna looked at Casey reproachfully; he had come so close to causing a fight on Mike's special day. Casey simply looked away, pretending not to catch the significance of her glance.

For the rest of the party, Amanda was scrupulously polite to Joanna, actively including her and, once or twice, even asking her opinion about what to do next. When at last the party came to a close, Joanna couldn't decide which had been worse: Amanda slighting her, or Amanda being so overwhelmingly solicitous.

That night, alone with Casey as they prepared for bed, Joanna asked him what he'd said to Burnett's wife.

Casey shrugged. "Nothing much. I reminded her that *I* have custody of Mike. And therefore, I determine with whom Mike associates and with whom he doesn't. She nobly decided that, for Mike's sake, she would have to be nice to you. She sees herself as the only constructive influence in Mike's life, and she considers it her duty, at any cost, to do what she can for him. She can't do that if she isn't allowed to see him."

Joanna shook her head. "Casey..." she cleared her throat, hesitating, because what she wanted to tell him was a criticism of what he'd done.

"What?" The question was pure challenge. His chest was bare, since he'd removed his shirt. He was sitting on the bed, getting out of his shoes and socks.

Joanna, already dressed in a short-sleeved nightshirt, was perched on the couch in the sitting area. "Well," she drew in a breath and forged on. "I don't know if threatening her really solves anything, that's all."

His mouth tightened as he stood up and tossed his shoes in the closet. "I did what I had to do. She left you alone after that, didn't she?"

"But it was descending to her level, in a sense, don't you think?"

"I told you what I think. It was necessary." He disappeared into the bathroom.

"But we want to learn to get along with her and Burnett," she said when he came back. "We don't want to go on forever digging at the same old wounds."

"She's not using you as a doormat, and that's final," Casey said. He yanked the zipper of his slacks down, stepped out of them and hung them in the closet. He turned and faced her, wearing only his snug white briefs.

"Now, can we drop it?" A trace of his usual humor sparked in his eyes. "It's bad enough that we have to deal with them from birthdays to Christmas to Easter and then back again. Let's leave them out of our bedroom, okay?"

Joanna, her bare legs gathered up under her on the couch, felt her face flushing—both with anticipation of what she knew would come soon, and with pleasure at the way he'd said *our bedroom*.

He held out his hand. She gladly jumped from the couch to take it. They went into his big bathroom together. He removed the contact lenses he wore and they brushed their teeth side by side in front of the huge mirror. They hadn't even rinsed the minty toothpaste from their mouths before they were kissing. Soon Casey was hoisting her up on the marble counter and showing her what erotic possibilities there were to be explored right there in front of the bathroom mirror between the double sinks.

All through the next week, Casey spent long hours at the airfield making up for lost time. Lillian came by often to take Mike for a few hours, or to drop him off at one of his friend's, so that Joanna could have the precious time she needed to work on the paintings for the gallery opening.

Late Wednesday afternoon, when Joanna was working on one of the studies of Casey at Chilly Lilly's and concentrating on capturing the play of artificial light on green tiles, Lillian returned with Mike. She asked Joanna to take an iced tea break with her out by the pool.

Joanna was so absorbed in her work that she almost requested a rain check. But then she glanced up and saw the anxious expression on Lillian's face.

"I sent Mike to his room to play," Lillian said. "I really do think we should talk."

Joanna blinked, coming out of her concentration on work and turning her attention to the real world. She smiled at Casey's mother. "Sure. Iced tea sounds great. Why don't you go on outside. I'll just clean up a little and be down in a jiffy."

Lillian was waiting for her at the glass table on the edge of the lawn, glasses of iced tea in front of her. Joanna sat down beneath the big umbrella and enjoyed a long, cool sip before urging with mock grimness, "Okay, what is it?"

"I'm not sure I should be here at all," Lillian began, clearly unsure. "I've thought about it and thought about it. And I'm still not sure I should be doing this."

"Okay," Joanna didn't know what else to say.

"It's about Amanda..."

"Yes. What about her?" Joanna said in a neutral tone.

"Well, I don't mean to speak ill of her, but she *has* been behaving terribly toward you."

Joanna focused on the shimmering reflection of the sun on the water in the pool. "We're two very different people," she said after a moment, trying her best to be fair. "Our personalities just don't mesh, I guess." Joanna looked back at Lillian. "Maybe in time—"

Lillian cut Joanna off with a slight wave of her hand. "She's extremely jealous of you, Joey, and you're sensitive enough to realize that."

"Well, yes. I've felt that."

"In part, she's jealous of the closeness you and I share. She longs to be the perfect daughter-in-law. It hurts her that I have such an easy, intimate relationship with you while I'm a little more reserved with her."

"I see," Joanna said. She hadn't really considered that Amanda might feel like an outsider when confronted with the closeness that Joanna and Lillian had shared for so many years.

"Furthermore," Lillian continued, "you were once engaged to her husband."

Joanna left off pondering Lillian's first point to deal with the old issue of her foolish engagement to Burnett. "But that was so long ago," Joanna protested. "And Burnett and I were so totally mismatched. It's absurd for Amanda to be jealous of that."

"Nonetheless, you and Burnett did once plan to marry. And Amanda's a little insecure about her relationship with Burnett right now."

Joanna sensed that Lillian was quickly approaching the crux of the matter. "You want to tell me why, is that it?" Joanna prompted. "But you're also worried that you'll be breaking Amanda's confidence if you talk to me about her relationship with Burnett."

"That's it exactly," Lillian replied. "But I've come here to ask you to keep on putting up with her, for the sake of the family. The way she's been behaving, that's a lot to ask. I feel that I should at least give you a reason to be tolerant of her."

Joanna reached across the table and squeezed Lillian's hand briefly. "Not if it's breaking a confidence. I'll keep trying to get along with her for you, and for Mike and Casey. I don't need any more reason than that."

Lillian's next words were grim. "Maybe you don't, but Casey does."

"I'll talk to him. I'll get him to get along with her for my sake and yours and Mike's." Joanna forced a laugh. "Whew. All this family intrigue is a lot of work. I didn't realize how easy I had it down in L.A., with only minor details to stew about, like how to pay the rent."

Lillian laughed with Joanna, but the laugh was short. "Seriously though, Joey, on Saturday I saw how fed up Casey is getting with Amanda and Burnett. If something isn't done, there's going to be a big, ugly split in this family. I can feel it."

Joanna was silent. She was thinking that any incipient split was partly Lillian's fault, for never confronting the fundamental hostilities between her two sons. She said, hesitantly, "Did you know that Burnett threatened Casey with a lawsuit to get custody of Mike?"

"Yes," Lillian admitted. She sounded infinitely sad. "Burnett told me his plans. I tried to reason with him, but he is so pigheaded. And then, of course, you and Casey announced your marriage and that ended that."

Joanna was silent. She was trying to keep from asking Lillian exactly how hard she'd tried to reason with Burnett on the issue of Mike's custody. But before she could diplomatically frame such a delicate question, Lillian went on.

"What I'm going to tell you is no secret in any formal sense. I mean, Amanda never specified that I not tell anyone."

"But she wouldn't like it if you did?"

"Probably not."

"Then I don't think you—"

Lillian didn't let her finish. "Joey, you need to know. You're part of the family. And you need to understand why Amanda is the way she is." Quickly, before Joanna could protest again, Lillian said, "Amanda wants desperately to have children. They've been trying for seven of the eight years they've been married. She's had difficulty conceiving. As a matter of fact, they've seen more than one doctor about the problem.

"A little over a year ago, she finally became pregnant. They were both ecstatic, though they told no one but me. They were waiting to get through the first trimester, to be sure everything was all right, before making any formal announcements. At eleven weeks she lost the baby."

Joanna looked out at the sparkling pool again. "Oh, Lord," she said, and she did feel real compassion for the perfect Amanda, whose deepest desire had so far eluded her

Joanna turned back to Lillian again. "So Amanda and Burnett want Mike for more reasons than I at first understood," she said.

"Yes." Lillian agreed. "They both long for children, and they're afraid they'll never be able to have them." Lillian paused to sip from her tea, before she added fervently. "Joey, I just know that in time Amanda and Burnett will accept the situation and decide to adopt a child. As soon as they do that, they'll let go of the idea of taking Mike away from you and Casey. Everything will work out fine. If only we can avert an all-out war in the meantime."

Joanna sighed, "I suppose you're hoping that I'll pass this information on to Casey."

Lillian smiled sheepishly. "Unless you want me to tell him."

Joanna considered her suggestion, and then realized she'd have to talk with Casey about it anyway, whether Lillian passed on the information first or not. "It's all right," she said after a moment. "I'll discuss it with him."

"Oh, thank you," Lillian said gratefully. "Maybe, if you two are incredibly tolerant, we'll avoid any awful confrontations next month," she said.

Joanna shot her a questioning look. "Next month?"

"Labor Day weekend, at Graeagle," Lillian told her.

Then Joanna remembered. The Graeagle weekend was an annual event with the Clintons. The whole family went. For three days. Joanna groaned inwardly at the thought: herself and Casey, Burnett and Amanda, Lillian and Mike, all sleeping under the same roof and sharing each other's company for seventy-two hours. It would be an exercise in tolerance, to put it mildly.

"I don't know, Lillian," Joanna began carefully. "Maybe this year we shouldn't push our luck."

Lillian's face fell. Joanna realized how much observing the family tradition meant to her mother-in-law.

"All right, count us in," Joanna said. "Somehow, we'll all manage to get along."

Chapter Ten

Casey didn't arrive home until late that evening. Running a small, private airfield was demanding. Rhonda Popper was willing to work in the office full-time for a pittance and plenty of flight hours, but the burden of most of the paperwork still fell on Casey's shoulders—a burden he accepted in order to keep costs down. The two weeks he'd taken off after the wedding had to be made up.

He found Joanna in her studio, where she was just finishing the second painting of him in the ice-cream shop. He came up behind her and kissed the back of her neck.

"Why is it that lately I find the smell of paint thinner erotic?" he teased.

She leaned back into his chest, holding her palette and brush out in front of her and studying the painting she'd just finished. "Because you're a man of taste and discernment," she told him. "Did you look in on Mike?" she asked.

"Uh-huh. He's asleep for the night."

"Did you eat?"

"You bet." He nuzzled her neck. "As a matter of fact, I'm ready for dessert."

She giggled, and thought how nice it was to have Casey's arms to look forward to every night. It was surprising, really, how easy she'd found it to integrate him and Mike into her life. If it wasn't for their family difficulties and the fear she had that something was troubling Casey, she would have called her life perfect.

She rolled her head against his chest until she could kiss his chin. "Tell you what. Why don't you let me clean up a little in here and I'll meet you in the bedroom in fifteen minutes."

He kissed her mouth, quickly. "Deal," he said, and left her alone.

Joanna cleaned her brushes and took a quick shower. She joined Casey with two minutes to spare. For a while, they lay side by side on the big bed, talking about the events in their respective days.

Finally, she told him about what Lillian had revealed about Amanda's longing for a child. There was a silence after she was done. Casey was lying on his side, facing her, his head resting on his bent arm.

He levered himself up on an elbow and asked, "So what's the point?"

Joanna blinked, surprised at his sudden curtness. Until then, she had been feeling so contented, savoring the clean scent of his skin and hair after his evening shower, enjoying the sound of his voice as he talked to her and anticipating the moment when one of them would reach out and touch the other with intimate intent.

She sat up, crossing her bare legs Indian-fashion and smoothing the hem of her nightshirt over them. "Well, Casey," she said, "the point is that Amanda's had a difficult time."

"So that makes it all right for her to treat you like dirt?"

"Well, no, but—"

"That's what my mother's saying, isn't it? She wants you to let Amanda walk all over you because poor Amanda can't have a child. And she wants me to sit by and let it happen."

"Casey, please. Don't be like this."

Suddenly, he was off the bed and pacing the floor. "Damn it. She should have come to me, not dragged you into it."

"Casey, she offered to talk to you herself."

"Sure she did." He stopped pacing long enough to glare at Joanna. "As soon as she'd finished laying it all on you. Because she knew I wouldn't be as sympathetic as you, she took advantage of her relationship with you, figuring maybe you could do a better job of getting me in line."

"Come on," Joanna slid off the bed and approached him. "You know how Lillian is. We've talked about it a hundred times. On our own wedding night, when I was the one complaining about her, you said it yourself: Lillian is who she is. She hates conflict. You can't suddenly expect her to act like someone else."

"It's not your problem," he said.

She looked at him, eye to eye. "It is very much my problem," she told him. "It has been ever since you talked me into marrying you." He stared back at her, and she saw a bleakness in his light eyes. "Casey, what is it?" she heard herself pleading. "What's bothering you?"

"Nothing." He turned away and went to the sitting area. He stood near the couch looking out the bay window at the sloping lawn and the quiet nighttime street.

Joanna drew in a long, deep breath. "You feel guilty, is that it?" she asked him, "For getting me involved in all this?"

"You're damned right," he said, still staring out the window.

"Casey," Joanna paused, wanting to frame her thoughts carefully. "It was wrong of me to say you talked me into marrying you. I chose to get involved. You may have pressured me, but I wouldn't have given in to that pressure unless I knew it was the right decision."

"It's a bad deal for you, all around," he said. "You can be a good sport about it, but we both know what's what in the end."

Joanna stared at his back, not knowing what to say to bring him out of this strange dark mood. She didn't know how to reach him when he was like this.

In their years as friends, Joanna had been the one whose moods had been erratic; she was the one who had had a tendency to brood. Casey was the one who never overreacted, never took things too seriously. He could be outrageous, but he was usually patient with the failings of others—unlike now when he had so abruptly become furious with his mother's actions. Never before had she seen Casey angry with Lillian for trying to avoid a fight. Dealing with this new volatility in him made her feel like she was dealing with a total stranger.

And ten minutes ago, she'd been thinking how comfortable and cozy they were together...

Casey turned away from the window and looked across the room at her. As he so often did before bedtime, he wore only his loose khaki slacks. He crossed his arms over his beautiful chest. "Are there any more dead babies I should know about so I can work on being more understanding when my brother and his wife treat my wife like a dart board?"

"Casey, that's a lousy thing to say," Joanna said. "It's not worthy of you at all."

"Isn't it?" He dropped his arms to his sides and approached her, his bare feet soundless on the thick close-woven carpet.

"Are you trying to pick a fight with me?" she challenged.

He stopped opposite her and very slowly reached out to smooth a swatch of hair back over her shoulder. The small gesture, in spite of her ambivalence toward him then, was like a signal. His hand whispered along her neck, and she was trapped in the awareness of the pleasure his touch could bring her.

"Joey," he said. "What makes you think I want to fight?" His eyes dared her, and the dare was all about the delight they could be sharing right this minute.

"You do this to me all the time lately," she accused halfheartedly.

Lazily, he undid the top button of her nightshirt, and then took the collar points and pulled them apart, so the tops of her breasts were revealed to him.

"Do what?" he asked.

"Make love instead of telling me what's going on inside you."

He undid another button, then looked from her breasts into her eyes. "What's going on inside me is I want to make love with you."

What could she say? He knew she would listen, if he chose to open up. But he didn't open up, and in the final analysis, that was his right.

His fingers moved nimbly, until her shirt was completely open. She tipped her head back, to watch his face, her eyelids heavy with building desire.

He cupped her bared breasts with his hands as his eyes held hers. Joanna sighed.

"I love it when you look like that," he said. "Your eyes all heavy, wanting me." He bent his head to her breast. She swayed on her feet, moaning aloud as he sucked a nipple into his mouth. She combed her fingers through his thick hair and held his head there, while he nipped and licked and blew cool air across the tender flesh, pleasuring her.

He stood up again and gathered her against his chest. His lips were breath-close. She strained toward them. He loosened his slacks and felt for her hand, guiding it to where she could feel the proud evidence of his hunger for her.

"This, at least," he said against her mouth, "is fine between us. Isn't it, Joey?"

"Oh, Casey..." Her hand closed around him, cupping him.

"Say yes," he whispered. "Say you like it."

"I do," she heard herself murmur. "I love it, I do..."

Then he gave her his mouth, kissing her deeply and with growing abandon until she felt she would melt there against him, melt into a molten pool of desire right there on the tan carpet six feet from his big, white bed.

Insistently, he pushed the nightshirt from her shoulders. She was nude for him except for her panties, which he soon removed as well.

Then he swung her up against his chest, carried her to the bed and laid her down on it. His eyes burned into hers as he took off the rest of his own clothes.

At last, gloriously naked, he joined her on the bed, loving her first with his mouth. Then, after she had touched heaven once, he entered her and together they found that magical place where mutual fulfillment overwhelmed them.

Later, as she held his head against her breast and lay sated, gazing up at the ceiling, she remembered about the Graeagle weekend.

"Casey?"

Languidly, he was tracing a figure eight on the smooth skin of her waist. "Um?"

"There was one other thing that Lillian mentioned..."

His lazily tracing finger grew still. "What?"

"The Graeagle weekend."

"What about it?"

"She expects us to go, that's all."

He raised his head and looked at her. "And you said we would."

"Well, except for the time you were overseas with the navy, you'd always gone before."

He rolled away from her to lie faceup, throwing an arm across his eyes. "This isn't before," he said.

"It's a month away," she tried optimistically, as if she was hoping the situation might change dramatically in that space of time.

"It's a bad idea," he said.

"Casey, I promised." Joanna didn't like herself very much at that moment. She knew she should have waited to consult him.

"It'll be a disaster," he said. "And Burnett and Amanda won't miss a trick when it comes to running you down."

"I'm an adult. I can take whatever they dish out."

He looked at her, moving his arm away from his eyes to his forehead. "You're just not in the pattern about this at all," he said, using a pilot's expression.

"What do you mean? I understand what's going on completely."

"They're chipping away at you, Joey. Little by little, they're trying to wear you down. They figure that you're the weak link in my claim on Mike."

"Oh, Casey. That's a little farfetched, don't you think?"

"No." The word was flat, unequivocal. "After what I saw at Mike's party Saturday, I don't think it's farfetched at all."

He went on, sounding weary and a little bitter, "Some things never change, and we're fools if we think that they can. When my father deserted us, Burnett was eleven. He took on the burdens of the man of the house then and he hasn't stopped trying to run all our lives since. My mother feels guilty; she always hesitates to criticize him because she knows she really leaned on him. She knows that without his business brains and willingness to work like a dog when he should have been out being a kid, none of us would be rich now."

He was staring at Joanna, that scary bleakness in his eyes again. "The hostilities between Burnett and me go so deep, the bottom would be impossible to reach, Joey. There *is* love there, but it's all wound up with resentment and anger. I've always had all the freedom he could never allow himself, and I've never used it the way he thought I should."

Casey's words rang too true for Joanna's peace of mind. She shivered a little. Then she sat up and dragged the throw cover from the foot of the bed, wrapping it around her bare shoulders. "You really think Burnett and Amanda are so diabolical that they would consciously try to break up our marriage?" she asked.

Casey had turned on his side, facing her. With hooded eyes he had watched her wrap herself in the blanket. He himself remained splendidly nude, cloaked only in his considerable male grace. "Conscious or unconscious," he said, "what's the difference if the outcome is the same?"

"The difference is that I can take it." Joanna leaned over and kissed him on the nose in an attempt to lighten the mood, which had grown much too somber for her liking.

In the past, it had always been Casey who lightened the mood, she thought. But somehow, their marriage had switched things around. More and more, Joanna played the role of the optimist.

"It's not fair to you," Casey said.

"I can handle it," she told him for what seemed like the hundredth time. "For Mike's sake, I can handle a heck of a lot."

"Right," he said. "For Mike's sake." Then, abruptly, he sat up and began swinging his legs off the side of the bed.

Joanna watched, puzzled at first, as he gathered his clothes from the rumpled pile on the floor and proceeded to put them on again. "You're going out?" she asked, when she realized what was happening.

"Not out." He zipped up his slacks and went to the chest of drawers opposite the foot of the bed. He found a T-shirt and pulled it over his head, then spoke again as he tucked the shirt into his pants. "I brought home a stack of log sheets this high. I should get to them."

"But Casey—"

"What?" He paused by the closet to cast her a rather impatient look over his shoulder.

"Well, we were talking about something that's important—and all of a sudden you've got work that can't wait."

"The subject seems pretty much played out."

"But we didn't even decide about the weekend at Graeagle."

"Sure we did," he said. "You decided about that way before you even thought of consulting me."

Joanna drew a deep breath. "Okay. I was wrong. I'll tell Lillian that we won't be going this year."

"Hell, no," he said, his tone a mockery of lightness. "The Graeagle weekend is a family tradition. And we can't go breaking with tradition, now can we?"

"Casey—"

"Look," he said. "We've run the subject of my family right into the ground and all the way to China. I'm sick and tired of it. And I do have work I need to do."

"It feels to me like you're running away," she said.

"Okay," he sighed. "I'm running away. And I have work to do."

"But Casey, I don't—"

He cut her off, fed up. "Just give it a rest, will you please, Joey?"

He came where she sat on the bed. He bent over to kiss her before leaving her for work she knew he'd invented. When she didn't immediately raise her face to his, he tipped her chin up with his hand. "Come on," he said. His touch was tender on the soft skin of her throat. "Let it be. Some things in life never get worked out."

Like what's bothering you? she thought, but didn't say. It would do no good to ask, anyway. He wouldn't tell her. And ironically, her desire to understand seemed to only drive a wider wedge between them.

"Smile?" he asked.

Obediently, she forced the corners of her mouth up. His lips met hers once, sweet and brief, and then he went downstairs.

Chapter Eleven

For Joanna, August passed in a sweltering haze of creative activity. The paintings for the gallery show seemed to almost paint themselves.

The paintings, at first studiously realistic, became more impressionistic, renderings of light and shadow, striking in their vividness, as Joanna let herself go.

Casey was busy, too, both with the airfield and with Mike. Still, he and Joanna found time to make love almost every night, and how good they were together in that most intimate of ways continued to take her breath away.

After the night they'd argued about the Greagle weekend, Joanna was careful to avoid the dangerous subjects that made her new husband turn away from her. She stopped asking him what was bothering him;

she remained scrupulously neutral whenever anyone mentioned either his brother or his sister-in-law.

More than once, Amanda dropped by on what she said was a whim. Because Joanna knew Burnett's wife always wanted to see Mike, she was able to avoid any trouble by just leaving Amanda alone with the boy.

Sometimes, during a rare quiet moment when her latest canvas wasn't consuming all her attention, Joanna would find herself wondering sadly what had happened to the old ease she and Casey had always shared. When she wasn't looking her best friend had faded away and left in his place a cordial stranger who treated her with thoughtful consideration and kindness during the day—and set her nights on fire.

But then she would rouse herself from the negative speculations and go back to work, or play with Mike, or look up to see Casey watching her. They'd exchange smiles, and she'd want to ask, What is it, what's happened to us? But she wouldn't, because she knew it would do no good at all.

On Thursday, August thirty-first, Joanna put down her brush for the last time before the opening of her show in Los Angeles on September eighth. Most of the paintings had already been flown down to the gallery the week before; all that remained to be transported were the last ones she'd completed. She and Casey could take those with them on Tuesday, when he flew her down so she could work with Althea on the finishing touches for the show.

Joanna stood back from the big canvas she'd just completed. The late afternoon sun came through the bay window behind her and picked up the red heat of the dying sun in the painting.

It was a rendering of a certain magical moment during that long-ago weekend at Graeagle when both she and Casey had been eighteen. She'd painted the Mill Pond with a single small rowboat out in the middle, turning slowly in a circle as the sun dropped behind the western hills. In the boat there were two figures, one at either end. The figures were Casey and Joanna; they weren't detailed enough for anyone looking at them to ascertain their genders, let alone the fact that they were a boy and a girl of eighteen at a moment of crossroads in each of their short lives.

Casey had been headed for the navy shortly after that. Joanna had been planning to marry Burnett in the fall, but would end up going to UCLA and becoming an artist.

Graeagle, now mostly a vacation and retirement community, had once been a logging town. The big pond where the logs once floated, waiting to be milled, was virtually deserted when Casey had led her out there with the intention of going for a sunset swim.

By plowing through a few willow stands and stomping doggedly in marshy grass, they finally came to a place that Casey had declared acceptable.

Casey had coaxed Joanna into the abandoned boat that he had found in the rushes. As she started to slide the oars through the rowlocks, he had signaled to her not to bother; he swam the boat out toward the middle of the pond, strong legs beating beneath the water, one hand on the stern to guide the boat.

Slow, lazy ripples had moved out from the bow before her, shot with the colors of the dying sun. Out in the center, it was still, a peaceful kind of quiet made more so by the slight bobbing of the boat and the soft slap of water against the sides.

Sleek and agile as an eel, Casey had glided up over the side and into the boat and had moved toward the back. Joanna naturally made the adjustment to his weight, moving forward a little and turning to face him, perching on the sailing thwart, while he took the seat in the stern.

The hot ball of the sun sunk halfway behind the mountains and hung there, bleeding its final colors into the darkening sky. Pale to the northeast, the moon seemed to be waiting for darkness and her chance to dominate.

Casey took an oar and gently dipped it in the water. The boat turned, slowly, in a circle, and the panorama of the pond, the sloping grassy land, the sentinel pines, the shadowy distant hills and the twilight sky were Joanna's to experience and know.

Then the swallows came, soaring effortlessly above, snatching unwary insects as they dipped and rose in strong and buoyant flight. Their occasional calls were unmusical, but the music in their flight alone was enough for Joanna.

The sun dropped from sight, leaving only an iridescent rim of pink and orange on the western horizon, and the swallows became like living shadows, wings spread in double chevrons against the dusky sky.

Joanna had felt transported in ecstasy by the sheer beauty of the world around her. She sat, the sketchbook that Casey had insisted she carry with her laid across her lap, her hands hooked beneath her pressed together knees. She drank it all in, as the night fell and the air cooled perceptibly against her sun-warmed skin.

"I'll miss you," Casey had said. He was on his way to the navy two weeks from that day.

Joanna, lowering her gaze from the sky, had looked at his face, shadowed across from her as he stopped his gentle circular rowing. The boat had stilled with Joanna facing the hills where the sun had gone.

"I'll miss you, too," she had said. She had felt, at that moment, an absolute confidence in the security of his friendship. She had felt that the boy across from her knew her exactly as she truly was, and accepted her without reservation. At that moment she had known she would not marry Burnett, and that she would go to Los Angeles after all....

Now, fourteen years later, the more mature Joanna turned abruptly from the painting embodying a moment of absolute affinity between herself and her best friend. She busied herself cleaning up, then she took a long, refreshing shower.

Out the small bathroom window, she could hear Casey and Mike splashing in the pool. She joined them after she'd finished her shower. She swam a few laps and then floated on a rubber raft in the scorching sun until Casey reminded her to either find some shade or slather herself in sunscreen.

That night Casey made love to her with an intensity and beauty even more stunning than all the incredible nights before. It seemed to Joanna that she became pure sensation. He explored and mastered every inch of her yearning body, bringing her once and then again to a shuddering satisfaction, cradling her close against him, and then starting all over again.

Finally, exhausted from delight, her head nestled in the crook of his arm and her legs entwined with his, she drifted toward a bottomless well of sleep.

"Joey..." his voice came to her, his breath playing across the crown of her head.

"Um?" She shifted a little, snuggling closer into his warmth against the air-conditioned coolness of the room.

"Joey, I..."

"Yes?"

Then there was a long silence, and the part of her mind that held on to a thread of consciousness knew she should prompt him, ask him to go on.

She forced sleep away, canted up on an elbow and pushed the mass of tangled hair away from her face. "What? Tell me."

For a moment, their eyes held, and she was sure that he was going to open up to her at last. She felt the beginnings of relief—and she felt dread.

Over the past weeks, she'd begun to fear more and more that the reason for the change in Casey was that, deep down, he didn't like being married. For Mike's sake, he was staying with it. But she was afraid that he'd call it off in a minute if the custody issue were resolved. He'd dared her to marry him; she'd accepted the challenge and now they were stuck with each other, for better or worse. For as free a spirit as Casey Clinton, Joanna feared, the bonds of matrimony felt too much like prison walls.

Casey was looking at her silently.

"Do you want out of this marriage, Casey?" she heard herself asking, her voice stark and low. "Is that it?"

"No," he said. "I don't. Do you?'

"No," she said.

They looked at each other across what seemed like a huge chasm of silence. Joanna wondered then what else she could do. When she asked what was wrong, he always said nothing. She hated the rote exchanges: Do you regret? . . . No, do you? . . .

"What did you want to say?" she asked then.

"Never mind." He pulled her down against his chest, and tugged the sheet over them. "It's late. We should get some sleep to be fresh for tomorrow."

Tomorrow, Joanna thought grimly, when they would be leaving for Graeagle and the annual family Labor Day weekend.

Joanna lay close to her husband and dreaded the next three days with all her heart. The feeling of foreboding had increased over the past weeks, every time the subject of the weekend had come up: when she'd marked the dates on the calendar in the kitchen, when she'd learned that Burnett and Amanda would definitely be going, when Amanda had called a few days ago to instruct Joanna on what groceries to bring. Joanna couldn't shake the growing certainty that seething hostilities would flare into out-and-out conflict given three days of proximity between the Clinton brothers and their wives.

She should cancel, she thought, no matter what a family stir her backing out would cause. Going when she felt like this was comparable to blithely boarding an airplane after having noticed an Uzi sticking out of the flight bag of the passenger in front of you.

Fitfully, Joanna turned over, pulling away from Casey and seeking the cool sheets on her own side of the bed. At her back, she felt Casey shifting too, turning away, to his side.

For a while, she lay staring at the dim reflection of her sheet-covered body in the mirrored closet door.

Joanna wanted to scream. Or to cry. Or to beg Casey to be honest with her.

But then she realized that what she needed to do was to stop driving herself crazy over things she could do nothing about. In the past, Casey would have been the first to point that out to her.

But, she told herself firmly, this isn't the past. This is the present. Casey and I are married. We both want it to stay that way, for Mike's sake, no matter what doubts Casey feels he can't share with me. We said we'd go to Graeagle, and that's exactly what we're going to do. It's going to be fine. It's going to be fun.

Resolutely, Joanna rolled over and invaded her husband's side of the bed. She wrapped herself around his back, spoon-fashion, and was extremely gratified when he reached for her hand, pulling her arm around him at the crook of his waist and entwining his fingers with hers.

The next morning they were packed and on the road by nine. At Casey's suggestion, they took the scenic route to Graeagle, through Grass Valley and up Highway 49. They turned off at Bassetts Station and took the Gold Lake Forest Highway, driving past spectacular views of the Sierra Buttes. Then they traveled down into the Lakes Basin, past all the dirt road turnoffs that led to campgrounds at the myriad small lakes tucked in among the tall trees and rugged hills.

Mike, seated in the back of Casey's Chevy Blazer along with the suitcases and the bags of groceries, kept up a steady, excited stream of chatter throughout most of the three-hour drive.

Someday, he explained, he'd stop in Downieville and pan for gold... When could they climb the Buttes?... Did Casey and Joey think probably there were deer at Deer Lake and horses at Horse Lake?... And what about Gold Lake, huh? Was there probably lots of gold, a treasure in gold there, didn't they think?

Then there was Sand Pond. They'd gone swimming there last year. Could they please go again this year, too?

Casey and Joanna took turns good-naturedly dealing with the boy's endless queries. Joanna rolled down the window after they'd left Grass Valley and relished the feel of the clean mountain air flowing over her face and tangling her hair.

The sky overhead was the summer-blue of Casey's eyes, pale, but vibrant with light. The few fat clouds were cotton-white, more reminiscent of an artist's idealized rendering than of anything that might actually produce rain.

As they turned onto Highway 89, the road that cut right through Graeagle where it lay nestled in the Mohawk Valley, Joanna happened to glance at Casey. He felt her eyes on him and gave her a quick smile and a wink.

Joanna sat back in her seat, temporarily content with the world and her place in it. The night before she'd made the resolution not to let her negative thoughts get the best of her. So far, it seemed to be working out just fine. She was on her way to a holiday weekend with two people she loved. Everything else, she'd cope with.

They arrived at the cabin at noon, before any of the others. Joanna climbed from the Blazer and stretched, loosening up the kinks from the drive. She gave herself a moment to appreciate the cabin, which lay at the crest of a sloping natural lawn of wild clover and Bermuda grass.

Joanna had always liked the cabin, which was really more like a country cottage. It was painted rust-red, as were most of the dwellings that had originally been owned by a company that had once run a profitable lumber mill in the town. The tin roof peaked high, so winter snow would slide off, and the rustic stone chimney dominated the outside wall toward the garage.

Lillian had inherited the property from a wealthy bachelor uncle, along with the money that she'd used to start up the family chain of ice cream-shops.

Behind her, Joanna heard Mike hit the ground at a run.

"Hold on," Casey ordered from the other side of the Blazer. "Where do you think you're going, kid?"

"Just across the street, Uncle Case. I gotta check out the Mill Pond, and find out if Megan came." Megan, Joanna had learned, was a girl Mike's age whose family had vacationed here the year before.

"That street is the highway," Casey said, "and you're not to cross it without adult supervision. And before you do anything, we need to unload the truck."

"Aw, Uncle Case..."

"Then you have to have a sandwich."

Mike groaned, a long, theatrical sound. "*Uncle Case...*"

Casey chuckled. "Do it and get it over with."

Dramatically slumping his shoulders, his tennis shoes dragging on the pebbled driveway, the boy went around to the rear of the truck where Casey handed him a bag of groceries.

Joanna smiled to herself as she got in line behind Mike to do her share of toting food and suitcases to the cabin. Casey had always been good with Mike, but invariably in the role of the indulgent uncle. When Emily died, Casey would no more have known how to keep the boy in line than Joanna would have known how to bring a navy fighter plane in on the postage stamp runway of an aircraft carrier.

But now, especially since the boy's scary bout with the flu in Los Angeles the month before, Casey seemed to have learned that being a parent wasn't all affection and indulgence. Sometimes doing what was right for a child was the hardest thing a parent could do, and often the child didn't like it one bit.

At this point, Joanna mused, Casey was completely capable of raising Mike on his own. His schedule was flexible, and he'd become accustomed to including the boy in his day-to-day existence.

If she and Casey hadn't ended up married, it would have been time for her to return to her own life in Los Angeles. Oddly, Joanna could hardly imagine herself going back to her apartment to pick up her old life. Somehow, imperceptibly, Casey's house had become her home and Casey and Mike a necessary part of her life.

Luckily for her, she thought with equal parts irony and guilt, Burnett and Amanda had made it imperative that Casey find a wife. Joanna chuckled to herself. The next time she longed to throw Amanda off the nearest available cliff, she'd simply remind herself that if it wasn't for Casey's brother and his wife, Joanna wouldn't be married to Casey now.

"What's that big grin about?" Casey asked, as he handed her a box piled with hotdog buns, paper plates and plastic flatware.

"Just thinking what a gorgeous day it is and what a lucky lady I am to be sharing it with my two favorite guys," she told him.

He grinned back at her. "That's what we love to hear." He passed her the keys to the cabin and she laughed as she juggled the bulky box in an effort to catch them.

Mike was waiting beneath the tin porch roof that ran along the front of the cabin like a high skirt. He was holding a bag of groceries, shifting impatiently from one foot to the other.

"C'mon, Joey. I got things to do!"

Obligingly, Joanna mounted the two steps and stuck the key into the lock beneath the old, yellowed porcelain knob.

The door swung open, and Mike edged past her, hurrying to the kitchen to set down his load and rush back out to the Blazer for more. Joanna took a minute to appreciate the interior, which to her was like somebody's fantasy of homeyness. The planked walls were painted in pale greens and gray-whites, and rag rugs were scattered over the fir floors. All the furniture seemed to have been handed down for generations—fat, faded and inviting. The sofa was upholstered in a rose-patterned fabric, with antimacassars on the arms and across the back.

Joanna followed Mike into the bright kitchen, where someone had added a handy pine-topped island and stenciled bunches of grapes in a row near the ceiling. The stencils were a new addition since the last time Joanna had visited the cabin. Joanna remembered that Lillian and Emily used to spend weekends here often, and remembered them talking about different changes they'd made. Joanna found the thought pleasing, of Emily and Lillian here together, supervising the installation of the island, or stenciling the walls. With a contented little grunt, Joanna set her box on the island next to the bag Mike had brought in before he'd trooped back outside for more.

Within an hour, they were completely unpacked and Mike, who'd made alarmingly short work of his sandwich, was off looking for Megan.

The boy had listened with growing impatience as Casey had reiterated that under no circumstances was he to cross the street alone to get to the Mill Pond. Visiting Megan's was allowed, since the girl's family rented a cottage on the same side of the highway as the Clinton cabin.

"Jeez, Uncle Case," Mike had finally interrupted. "I promise, I promise. I won't cross the street alone. Now, it would be totally excellent if I could please get going now."

At last, the boy had been released. Casey and Joanna had finished their own lunch at a more leisurely pace. Then Joanna had volunteered to clean up while Casey went out and replenished the woodpile.

Thunk. Joanna looked out the kitchen window to see Casey sink his ax into a big chunk of cedar. Joanna decided she felt cooped up. She'd lingered in the kitchen when she could be outside among the pines. She hung the dish towel back on its peg by the window and climbed the steep back stairwell to one of the trio of second-floor bedrooms.

In the room that she and Casey would share, she found her blank sketchbook along with a few soft pencils. Then she hurried back down the stairs and out into the early-afternoon sun. She joined Casey in the backyard and perched on a log beneath a cedar tree at the edge of the clear, grassy space that defined the cabin's backyard.

Flipping to a clean page, she spent more time trying to capture the impression of the sky seen through a web of pine needles, trying to depict the lambency of random rays of sun peeking through the branches. It wasn't easy to do without using color, but she found her interest and absorption growing.

Joanna drew the trail that wound off into the woods, trying to capture the way the shadows thickened, as the branches of the trees meshed overhead. She drew the woodpile, with the garage in the background. And then, on the next page, quickly, just the ax head as Casey brought it down with a thunk on a hunk of wood.

Then she started on sketches of Casey, of his arms, lifting up and then bringing down the ax. Of his feet, in a pair of old laced up boots, planted in a pile of wood chips. Of his back, beautifully muscled and dewed with sweat as he rhythmically lifted and brought down the ax.

And then Casey stopped, turning toward her and wiping his forehead with the back of his gloved hand. "Whew. Good for what ails you."

She caught that, too—the satisfied tiredness in his hard body, and the moment when his hand blotted his forehead.

"Let me see," he teased, knowing she wouldn't show him. After all the years they'd been friends he was well aware of her personal creative eccentricities.

"Uh-uh. Sketching's private. Always," she muttered, and went on drawing. When she glanced up, he was stacking the wood in the lean-to box against the garage. She flipped the page and drew him throwing the wood in, her strokes quick and sure, not needing to look up at him again after one glance.

As her fingers flew over the white paper, a shadow fell across the sketchbook. Joanna looked up and found Casey standing over her, his work gloves in his hands. "I thought you were through working for a few days." She could hear the smile in his voice, though the midafternoon sun behind him made his grin hard to see.

She shaded her eyes against the glare and grinned right back, thinking that maybe this weekend would turn out to be just what they needed after all. "Bad habits die hard."

He bent quickly and set his gloves on the log. As he stood up again, he feinted for the sketchbook. "Let me see..."

She giggled, yanking it away and putting it behind her back. "No way, Casey Clinton."

"If you're going to draw pictures of me with my shirt off, I've got a right to take a look."

"Uh-uh." She stood up, stepping backward over the log. He advanced on her, drawing his eyebrows together to show her he meant business.

"Come on, Joey."

She backed away. "No."

"Yes." He advanced.

"No." She curved around and began backing toward the house.

"Yes." He followed.

"No!" She broke and ran for the back step, clutching her sketchbook and pencils, laughing out loud.

He brought her down to the sweet grass, in the middle of the yard. They wrestled together for possession of the sketchbook, more in fun than in earnest.

"Let me go!" Joanna cried.

"Give me that," Casey demanded.

"No."

"Yes..."

"No..."

"Yes."

Finally, with a huffing pretense of great effort, Joanna sent her sketchbook and pencils sailing over her head. She and Casey ceased their mock struggles as they heard the sketchbook land on the porch and saw the pencils bounce on their erasers and roll down the steps.

"Now you've done it," Casey said.

Joanna squinted up at him. "Done what?" He had captured both her hands and held them over her head. His sweaty, bare chest heaved against her breasts.

"Forced me to choose," he said.

She squinted even more, her expression bemused.

"To choose," he explained, "which I want more. To look at pictures of myself with my shirt off—"

"Or?"

"To keep rolling around in the grass with you."

"It's a tough choice," she conceded.

"But I think I'm ready to make it."

Joanna fell in with his game, squirming a little, just to make the choice more interesting. "Take your time," she advised, her voice grown somewhat husky. "Give it lots of thought."

With his thumbs, he rubbed the sensitive inner skin of her arms, where he held them captive against the grass. "Right." Then he repeated after her, as if trying to remind himself, "Give it lots of thought..."

"You always did have a tendency to rush into things," she teased.

He moved his head just enough to shade her face from the glaring brightness of the sun. She could see his expression then; he was pretending to look incredulous. "Me? Rush into things?"

"Yes, you."

"Never."

"Always."

"Uh-uh."

"Uh-huh."

He shook his head.

She nodded hers.

Then both of them burst into a silly fit of giggling.

And then the giggling passed as, enticingly, Casey touched her lower lip with the very tip of his tongue. And then very lightly he bit the place he'd licked. And then he started nibbling all around her mouth, little soft quick kisses.

Joanna was captivated, as she always was when Casey's lips met hers. Until Casey had started regularly kissing her, she'd never realized that it could be so much fun.

Half the fun, of course, was kissing Casey back—which Joanna immediately began doing, stretched out on the grass under his damp, strong body beneath a hot late-summer sky.

She was just thinking how lovely it would be if they could just lie here forever, kissing lazily and pleasurably and letting the rest of the world take a hike, when the kitchen's screen door banged shut and footsteps could be heard on the porch.

The footsteps came to an abrupt halt. Joanna heard the sound of a soft feminine gasp. Then she heard a man clear his throat.

Casey swore feelingly against Joanna's mouth, and slowly raised his head. Joanna craned her neck and saw Burnett and Amanda standing side by side on the porch.

"'Lo, Big Brother," Casey said, then nodded at Burnett's gaping wife. "Amanda." Taking his sweet time about it, Casey backed off of Joanna, pushing himself to his knees.

Joanna scuttled to a sitting position. Then, taking her cue from Casey and realizing they'd done nothing at all to be ashamed of, she began casually plucking lawn burrs and grass from her shirt and hair.

"Well," Joanna said after a moment, when no one else seemed disposed to speak. "Did you two have a nice ride up? We took Highway 49. It was beautiful." She stood up, and brushed off her cutoff jeans. "Casey's already fixed us up with plenty of wood. Do you need some help toting things in from your car?" At that moment, Joanna noticed that the first button of her top had come undone. She decided not to button it up; that would only draw attention to it.

"Where is Mike?" Burnett said in a tone full of self-righteous reprimand.

Casey stood up, and went to the log at the edge of the yard to get his work gloves. "He went looking for Megan—his friend from last year."

"Alone?" Amanda asked.

"Yes. Alone." Casey slapped his gloves against his bluejeaned thigh, perhaps to rid them of slivers, but more likely to defuse his annoyance with his sister-in-law for her perennial attitude of pained reproach.

"My God," Burnett said, "That's the highway out there, not a hundred yards from the front door."

That was true, of course, but it was also Graeagle's main street, and as such hardly as dangerous as Burnett made it sound.

"Mike knows he's not to cross it alone," Casey said.

"He's six years old," Burnett accused.

"And very responsible." Casey pointed out.

The two brothers glared at each other. Then Burnett said with infinite patience. "It's simply not acceptable, Casey. You've completely ignored your obligations as a guardian while you..." He paused, as he presumably sought the most tactful way to describe what Joanna and Casey had been doing. "*Wrestled* with Joanna. What if Mike had seen you?"

Joanna looked down at her tennis shoes. Three whole days of this, she thought grimly, and then began casting about for some way to defuse the growing tension. She looked up at Burnett with a blinding smile.

"Well, Burnett," she said, "I guess if Mike had seen us he might have discovered that married people sometimes giggle and kiss each other. Then we'd have done our best to help him accept that."

"This is no time to be glib, Joanna," Burnett intoned. Joanna faced him refusing to lose her smile.

Over by the log, Casey chuckled. "Ease off, Big Brother," he said. "Joey's got it exactly right."

Then Casey sauntered over to Joanna's side. He put his arm around her. She looked at him, and saw that he'd come to the same conclusion she had. If they were going to make it through the weekend, they'd need a sense of humor and a willingness to bend.

"Maybe we got a little carried away," Casey said, "but there's still nothing wrong with people who love each other kissing."

Joanna's heart expanded. *People who love each other*... What a lovely ring that had to it. Of course, she knew how Casey meant it. Nonetheless, it sounded wonderful.

Casey squeezed her shoulder. Joanna smiled at him—and at that moment, she had a dazzling insight. An insight that left everything exactly the same, and yet changed the world completely.

Joanna realized she would always remember this precise instant. It was the moment when all the confusions and pain of the last weeks suddenly made sense. The truth had come to her at last. She at last realized that she had fallen deeply, irrevocably in love with her best friend.

On the porch, Burnett went on complaining about the way his nephew was being raised, and Amanda interjected occasional breathless agreements with her husband's diatribe.

The hot September sun shone down. The warm wind sighed gently around them, like the tender breath of a peaceable giant. From a nearby tree, a blue jay squawked, in counterpoint to Burnett's harangue.

Joanna memorized it all, and would remember the moment always.

The minute Joanna confessed her love to herself, she was assailed by conflicting impulses.

She longed to shout it out loud—shout it over the top of the tallest pine, out into the sky the color of Casey's eyes, beyond the clouds that were too beautiful to ever bring rain.

She wanted to be alone, and very quiet. She wanted to be in some secret place where no one would find her and where she could sit and savor what had happened to her. She longed to just turn the magic over and over in her mind and heart.

She wanted to go somewhere immediately with Casey, and make mad, passionate love to him until he swore he loved her back...

Until he loved her back...

Reality hit her like a physical blow.

Casey didn't love her, not in the way she realized she loved him. That was the problem.

And therein lay her pain.

One part of her mind commanded, *You must tell him at once.*

And another voice warned, *You must never tell him...*

Joanna stood there in the sun with Casey's arm around her and experienced a sense of both elation and despair.

Then a child's voice called from inside the house, "Hey, you guys, where are you? Grandma's here!"

Burnett hastily curtailed his tirade as Casey shouted, "We're out back!"

Mike burst through the screen. "Megan got braces. She'll be over later. Grandma's bringing her stuff in and we're s'posed to help."

Amanda knelt in front of Mike, the skirt of her summer dress pooling out around her like the petals of a flower in bloom. "Haven't you got a kiss for your Aunt Amanda?"

Dutifully, Mike complied. Casey's arm slipped off of Joanna's shoulder, and he took her hand. "Come on. We'll go around the side of the house." Joanna allowed herself to be tugged along, still half in shock from the awesome insight that she was madly, totally in love with her best friend.

Chapter Twelve

That night, they barbecued a huge flank steak that Amanda had carried, soaking in its savory marinade, on her lap through the whole trip to Graeagle. The au gratin potatoes, Amanda had had the foresight to make ahead of time; they only needed to be browned in the oven. The crisp green beans had been cut in advance, bagged and put in the picnic freezer so they'd stay fresh on the trip. Amanda simply put them on to steam when the time was right.

Joanna and Lillian were allowed to cut up the salad—for which Amanda had prepared a special dressing, of course.

For dessert, Amanda had baked a cake. Everyone praised the food. Amanda smiled modestly and said it was nothing, nothing at all. She'd always loved to cook.

Later, after Mike had taken his bath and been put to bed out on the screened-in side porch, time crawled for a while. There was no television or radio in the cabin. When Casey, Burnett and Emily were children, Lillian had forbidden such entertainments in Graeagle. She told them it was character building to have to entertain themselves for at least a few days out of the year. Somehow, the rule had become a tradition.

Sitting on the fat couch with the cabbage rose upholstery, lost in ruminations about her newfound love and still feeling unsure about how to deal with it, Joanna found herself longing for the reassuring sound of canned laughter; it would help her forget her confusion and provide a neutral focal point for a family that might otherwise end up at each other's throats.

But then Amanda discovered an ancient family album in the drawer of a pine desk.

"Oh, now, isn't this incredible," Amanda said with enthusiasm. She peeled back the cracked cardboard cover and looked down at the first page. "Oh, this is old, really old. Look at these *dresses,* Lillian."

"That was my Uncle Peter's album," Lillian said. "He gave it to me shortly before he died, and so I brought it up here, to the house that he left to me."

Amanda immediately squeezed herself between Lillian and Joanna on the couch. She turned the pages slowly, reverently, and Lillian explained that the stiff, stern people in the first yellowed photographs were her own grandparents and aunts and uncles, who had come to California at the turn of the century.

"That's Grandpa Lambert." Lillian pointed to an imposing, severe-looking man who bore a striking resemblance to Burnett. "Grandpa Lambert was a wanderer, always moving West and taking his family right along with him. Grandma used to say if the Pacific Ocean hadn't been in the way, Grandpa never would have stopped."

Lillian pointed to the faces of her grandfather's children. "There's my father, John Lambert. And here's Uncle Peter, the one who owned this cabin." She chuckled. "Uncle Peter was a character. He never married because he said that a woman would have to be a damn fool to put up with him—and he wanted nothing to do with fools. He made his fortune in oil down in Bakersfield, and because Graeagle was famous for its golf courses, he bought this place so he could come up here to play golf. Uncle Peter loved music," Lillian went on, and her voice was dreamy. "We used to visit him down south when I was growing up and I'd sit with him out on the porch of his great big house at sunset and he'd play gold rush songs on his harmonica—*My Darlin' Clementine* and *Oh, Susannah* . . . I loved those nights."

Lillian's musing voice continued as Amanda turned the pages, and the sepia-toned photographs gave way to ones of black and white. Paul Lambert met and married Rose Adair. They had one child, Lillian, who then figured prominently throughout the next several pages. It was clear from the photographs that Uncle Peter, single and childless, had doted on his niece.

Hemlines rose, bathing costumes became swimsuits, and Lillian Lambert grew to womanhood.

Joanna felt Casey's hand brush her shoulder. She glanced up to see him leaning over the back of the couch behind her, looking at the photographs with them, just as Burnett was doing from down at the other end of the couch near Lillian.

Casey caught Joanna's eye when she turned. They shared a quick exchange of glances, a flash of a smile, and Joanna's heart picked up its rhythm. She wondered if everyone could see it beating so rapidly against the light cotton dress she'd changed into for dinner.

But no one was looking. They were all staring at the album and listening to Lillian. "This is the house in Bakersfield...That's me in my Easter dress when I was seven...Me learning how to play golf...My eighth-grade graduation...Christmas the year I finished high school..."

Joanna dragged her attention back to the photographs in time to see the picture of Casey. While it looked like Casey, clearly it couldn't be since it had been taken well over thirty years before. After a moment, Joanna realized it must have been Casey's father, standing out behind the cabin with a young, radiant Lillian at his side and a baby in his arms.

"Edward," Lillian said softly. She laid a hand on the picture, and touched the man's face. "Right after you were born, Burnett. He was so proud to be a father."

Burnett's voice burned with bitterness. "He had a hell of a way of showing it."

Lillian sighed. "We were very young."

"He deserted his family."

Lillian looked at her older son. "That was a long time ago. And he's been dead for seventeen years."

Joanna stared at the old picture of the man who smiled so rakishly into the camera. Just like Casey, she thought—in looks at least. And she understood a little better the age-old animosities between the staid Burnett and his reckless younger brother who looked so much like the father who had forsaken them.

Quickly, Amanda turned the page. "Oh, look," she said with contrived brightness, pointing to a picture of three children sitting on a rumpled chenille bedspread. "That's all three of you, I'll bet."

"Yes," Lillian pointed at each small face in turn. "Burnett and Casey and our Emily. That was right before Uncle Peter died and we moved to Sacramento to make a new start."

That was the last picture. Amanda closed the album and then stretched elaborately.

"Well, all this mountain air has just tired me out," she said. "I think it's time we turned in."

Nobody argued. Lillian was probably ready for bed, perhaps Burnett was, too. Casey and Joanna were being studiously agreeable. There were seventy-two hours to live through without incident, and they had survived approximately nine of them so far.

It took a half an hour for everyone to get their turn at the cabin's single bathroom, but it was still before ten when the house fell quiet for the night.

Casey and Joanna's small room had one lovely feature, a lace-curtained bow window that overlooked the backyard. Casey was standing, shirtless and barefoot, by the window, looking out at the moonlit clear space behind the cabin when Joanna returned from brushing her teeth.

She hung her robe on a peg behind the door. Then she went, without speaking, to the bedside lamp and switched it off. He glanced at her, then back out the window.

"Easier to see out in the dark," she explained.

Casey nodded. "It's so peaceful here," he said. "I've always liked that about this place."

Joanna stood by the darkened lamp, her love like a living thing wrapped around her heart, something tender and soft and very young. It was wonderful right at that moment, just to hold love inside her and know that it lived.

Casey turned from the window again. He stood looking at her. His back was to the pale spill of moonlight from outside, so that, as on the night he had convinced her to marry him, she couldn't see his features.

Faintly, below the window, she could hear the little peepings and chirpings of the night creatures in the grass and in the woods beyond.

"There's room at this window for two," Casey said, and though she couldn't see his smile, she could hear it in his voice.

Joanna walked around the foot of the old four-poster bed to reach his side. They faced each other, in front of the window, and he smoothed her hair back over her shoulder, the way he always did.

"This is pretty," he said of her soft cotton nightgown.

"I bought it for this weekend," she told him, her tongue suddenly feeling awkward in her mouth.

Soon they would climb beneath the old quilt on the four-poster bed. They would do all the wonderful things they'd been doing since the week after their wedding. But everything would be changed. Now there wouldn't be a single corner of her heart that the man standing in front of her didn't hold, unknowingly, in his hands.

Perhaps now would be a good time to tell him . . .

But, oh Lord, if he really wanted out of the marriage, telling him she was in love with him would only make things worse.

Unable to wrap her lips around the words *I love you,* but also unable to keep silent at that moment, Joanna began explaining what really didn't need to be explained at all. "I bought it two weeks ago." She smoothed the collar of the nightgown. "It seemed appropriate, with the whole family so close, to wear a real nightgown. Instead of just shirts and slips . . . you know?"

He nodded, his shadowed expression solemn, as if her stammered unnecessary words had been pearls of wisdom. "Well, it's very pretty."

"Thank you."

"You're welcome."

They looked at each other. Somewhere out in the woods, an owl hooted. Joanna jumped, then giggled nervously. "It's so quiet."

"Like I said, peaceful," Casey's voice held a teasing note.

"Yes. Peaceful."

Joanna wondered vaguely if being in love also made one incapable of intelligent conversation.

"I think it's going pretty well so far, don't you?" she tried bravely.

His eyebrows drew together. "It?"

"The weekend. Burnett. Amanda. Everything." The stilted words were out before she remembered that

Burnett and Amanda were a forbidden subject, one she'd been careful to avoid with Casey the past few weeks.

But, miraculously, Casey didn't shut her out or turn away. Instead, he chuckled. "You were incredible, out in the backyard."

Joanna gulped, her face flushing with pleasure at such praise. "I was?"

"Uh-huh. I'll never forget it. You, picking burrs from your hair and trying to button up your shirt without anyone noticing, chattering away about the scenery on the drive up."

"We didn't do anything wrong," Joanna said.

"Hey," he reminded her, "I'm on *your* side."

"Well, sometimes they just—" Joanna couldn't find the words.

"I know," Casey said, signaling that the subject was better left closed. He pulled her head to his shoulder, and put an arm around her, turning them both toward the window.

For a time, they just stood like that, looking out at the trees, while Joanna suffered—and gloried—in her unspoken love.

So many things cried out to be discussed. In those few short peaceful moments in front of the window, Joanna knew they could not go on forever with a tacit avoidance of forbidden subjects. Silence could not take the place of real communication.

Now was not the time to get everything out in the open, not when the primary objective for the weekend was simply to survive it without a major family fight. But the time for total honesty was coming. Perhaps next week while they readied her show in Los

Angeles, or when they returned to Sacramento in the middle of the month. Perhaps then Joanna would tell Casey of her love.

And she would badger and beráte and plead and do whatever was necessary to get him to open up about what was bothering him. Then together they'd face whatever ugly truth he revealed. They were bound together, for Mike's sake. And for Mike's sake, and their own, they deserved the best, most truthful relationship that two caring individuals could create.

"Are you dropping off on me?" Casey teased in her ear.

She turned, and slid her arms up his bare chest, hooking them around his neck. "Must be all the fresh air," she teased back, remembering Amanda's words earlier that evening.

As she stood with her chin tipped up to him, Casey kissed her. It was a slow, deep kiss. At the touch of his lips, Joanna forgot that there was anything but pleasure in the world.

It was even better when you knew you were in love, she thought giddily, as he walked her backwards and fell with her across the high old bed.

But then, beneath them, the old springs complained—loudly. Casey pulled away and looked down at her, a pained expression on his face that their lovemaking would be accompanied by squeaky springs. Both of them laughed like naughty children—until they heard something hit the floor in the room next door and both realized exactly whose room shared a wall with their own: Burnett's and Amanda's.

"Oh, no..." They mouthed the words in unison.

"We could try the floor," Joanna suggested helpfully, though the single small rag rug didn't look inviting at all.

Casey laughed. "Lord, you are a good sport," he said.

"That's me," she told him gamely, "good old Joey, willing to try anything—once." But both of them knew the mood was spoiled. They couldn't make love and enjoy it knowing they might be overheard.

"Come on." He pulled her to her feet, drew back the quilt and urged her to get in the bed. All the while, he was shaking his head. "How I ever let you talk me into this mess, I'll never know."

"It's for the sake of the family," she reminded him.

He took off his jeans and slid in beside her, "Isn't that what they said in *The Godfather?*"

She nudged him in the ribs. "Stop it. Think of Amanda's cooking."

He molded himself around her back. "I am. And it's great. But if she tells us all one more time how she carried that flank steak on her lap all the way up here, I'll—"

"You'll smile politely and listen, that's what you'll do."

"I'm trying, Joey. I really am," he breathed in her ear.

"I know." She turned her head and kissed him lightly on the chin. "And you're doing great. Just watch. It's going to be fine. We're going to have a pleasant family weekend and we'll all go home on Monday feeling good because not a single ugly word had been said."

Chapter Thirteen

The strained, uneasy truce between the Clinton brothers and their wives lasted through Saturday, primarily because Casey and Joanna ceaselessly conceded to the wishes of the other two.

Casey wanted to drive over to the nearby community of Blairsden for breakfast at the River Pines Inn—but Amanda had already planned her special Belgian waffles with sour cream and strawberries. They ate the waffles.

Casey and Joanna thought of taking Mike back to the Lakes Basin to swim at Sand Pond, near Lower Sardine Lake. Burnett thought the boy would learn more if they visited the gold mining museum at Plumas-Eureka State Park, just a few miles away. They visited the museum.

Later in the afternoon, Casey urged Joanna to go for a swim with him in the Mill Pond. But Burnett wanted his brother's company on the golf course. Casey played golf.

A minor tiff between Joanna and Amanda occurred when Joanna decided to go swimming after all, and to take along Mike and his friend, Megan.

"What a lovely idea," Amanda remarked when Mike had dashed out to the side porch to pull on his swim trunks and Joanna was poised at the back stairwell. "I'd love to go myself, but there's just so *much* I have to do to get dinner prepared."

Joanna obediently picked up her cue and asked what she could do to help.

"Don't be silly, Joey, you know how you are in the kitchen."

Joanna thought a moment. Amanda's needling remark was just another in a never-ending series of similar remarks, but something in Joanna rose up this time and refused to simply let it pass. She said carefully, "No, Amanda. I don't know how I am in the kitchen. Why don't you tell me?"

At that moment, Lillian came in from the back porch where she'd been reading on the old Stickley couch beneath the kitchen window. Amanda blushed. "Oh, Joey, I've offended you. I forgot how sensitive you are."

"You haven't offended me," Joanna said. "How could you have offended me? You haven't said anything yet."

Lillian went to the ancient refrigerator and brought out a pitcher of iced tea. She busied herself pouring herself a glass.

While Lillian's back was turned, Amanda nodded significantly in her mother-in-law's direction. "Now is not the time for an argument, Joey," she said.

Amanda had a point, Joanna silently admitted. It would be best just to let it go. But the strain of the past twenty-four hours was beginning to show. She heard herself saying instead, "Amanda, I simply asked you what you meant when you said 'you know how you are in the kitchen, Joey.' I'd just like an answer, that's all."

Amanda refused to give one. Instead, she shot Joanna an admonitory look, clearly telegraphing how insensitive it was of Joanna to make trouble in front of dear Lillian. Then she rushed to Lillian's side. "Here, Mother. Let me cut you a nice, fresh lemon slice to go with that."

Lillian said, "No, thank you, Amanda. I prefer it with sugar."

"But lemon is so much better for you."

Lillian nodded. "You're absolutely right. But I don't like lemon."

Amanda looked puzzled. "But how could you not like lemon?"

Lillian chuckled. "I don't know, Amanda. But it's not something I lie awake at night worrying about."

"Let me just cut you a slice. Just taste it, and I'm sure you'll find it much more to your liking than sugar."

Lillian said, very patiently, "Amanda, I'm fifty-nine years old. I have tasted lemon before, and I don't like it in my iced tea."

Amanda said, "Oh."

At that point, Lillian ladled two spoons of sugar into her glass and grinned at Joanna who remained by the stairwell. Joanna herself was realizing that the absurd exchange over the lemon had, at least temporarily, eliminated her urge to confront her sister-in-law.

"I hope I haven't interrupted anything," Lillian said, casting Joanna a quick look of understanding.

"Interrupted anything?" Amanda asked, innocent as a crafty child. "What in the world could you be interrupting? Joey was just on her way upstairs to put on her swimsuit. She's taking Mike and Megan over to the pond."

"That's right," Joanna said, thinking grimly, only forty-eight hours to go. "Want to come, Lillian?"

"No, no, you go ahead. I'll just go back outside and finish my thriller."

Because the water at the Mill Pond was too cold for real swimming, the children played in the shallows while Joanna chatted with a local artist who'd set up his easel not far from where Mike and Megan were splashing around in the water.

Dinnertime, once again, consisted of Amanda playing chef and Lillian and Joanna being allowed to help out. Tensions increased after Mike went to bed and the five adults were again left with the mountain silence and one another's company.

Later, when Casey and Joanna lay tucked beneath the quilt in the squeaky four-poster, Joanna asked Casey how the golf game had gone.

"Just more of the same," he said after a moment.

"Meaning?"

"Meaning Burnett is still waiting to hear about our divorce."

Joanna, who had been lying with her back against him, rolled over and canted up on an elbow. "He said that?" The question came out sounding odd, because she'd started it at a normal volume and then had uttered the last word in a strained whisper when she realized who might possibly be listening on the other side of the wall.

"What's the matter?" Casey asked, his voice suddenly sharp. Joanna realized the strain of having to put up with Burnett and Amanda on a round-the-clock basis was beginning to affect him, too. "It's not as if that's news."

"Keep your voice down." She said this in a whisper, but it came out as a low hiss.

For a moment, he just lay there. She thought he was watching her, but because it was dark in the room and his back was to the window, she couldn't be sure. Then, so fast it startled her a little, he threw back the covers. "I've got to get out of here."

"Casey, wait—"

He pulled on his jeans and buttoned them up. Then he slid his feet into a pair of slip-on canvas shoes.

"I'm sorry," she said.

"Don't be sorry," he told her. "You didn't do anything." He was whispering now, too, his voice sounding as furtive and guilty in the darkness as her own.

"I spoke harshly. I didn't mean to."

"It's not your fault," he told her, still whispering. "None of this is your fault." He was already at the door.

"Don't leave." She was halfway out of the creaking bed. "Running away isn't the answer."

He threw out a hand to stop her from coming any closer. "I'm not running away. I need a little time alone, that's all."

"Yes, you are." Absurdly, Joanna felt the tears gather behind her eyes. "You're always running away. Ever since you married me, you've been running away any time things get too heavy for you."

"Joey, you don't understand," he said.

"Then *explain* it to me," she begged.

"I can't." His whisper held a pleading note in it, too. "Not here, Joey. Not now."

"Then when?"

There was a cavernous silence, then he murmured, "Soon."

She knew she should stop pushing him, but somehow she couldn't. "When? After this nightmare of a weekend is over? After my show opens in L.A.? After the holidays? After Mike's away in college? When?" Joanna felt the traitorous tears, pooling over, running down her cheeks.

"Oh, God, Joey," Casey said. He took a step toward her. "I'm sorry. I never meant—"

But Joanna knew if he touched her, it would be her undoing. She'd blurt out her love for him right then, in a tortured whisper, drowning in tears and pain. It would not be the way she had hoped to tell him.

She drew herself up. "No, please. Don't touch me." Casey froze where he was. Joanna swiped the tears away. "You're right. What we probably both need more than anything now is a little space."

He stood looking at her, a dark shape between the door and where she sat crouched at the foot of the bed. "You want me to go, then?" he said finally.

She forced a smile. "Nothing can be solved tonight, right?"

"Right."

"So you go on, take a walk . . . or whatever . . ."

"You're sure?"

"Yes, I'd like some time alone."

"All right." But then he didn't immediately leave. He added, "Joey, I'm sorry about this whole damn mess. You can't know how sorry."

"Don't be. It's no more your fault than mine."

"Yes it is. Us getting married was my idea—but we've been over this a thousand times."

"Exactly," Joanna said. "So go for a walk."

"I'll be back soon," he said.

"Take your time."

Joanna kept her brave smile until the door closed behind him. Then she wrapped her arms around the post at the foot of the bed and leaned her head against the smooth carved surface of the wood. She wanted to cry, but all her tears seemed to have deserted her. She felt only a bottomless weariness.

After a while, she slipped back beneath the covers and lay staring out the window at the moonwashed starry sky and the tall shadows of the pine trees on the surrounding mountains. She reassured herself that there was only Sunday and Monday till noon to get through now—they were halfway home. And as soon as they were away from the prying ears of Burnett and Amanda, she and Casey would get everything out in the open.

Joanna closed her eyes. Everything will be fine, she told herself. And then she felt the tears rising up again—because she didn't really believe that everything would be fine at all.

She had no idea what time Casey came back to bed, but when she awoke Sunday morning he was there.

When she opened her eyes, she found him watching her. He smiled at her.

"'Morning," he said, and the word was like a signal passing between them.

She repeated it to him and in doing so, without mentioning the night before, she was tacitly agreeing to his unspoken suggestion: they would leave what had happened between them last night unexamined—at least until they'd left Graeagle.

As they dressed to go downstairs, they were careful of each other, as if each considered the other in danger of breaking.

Joanna dressed in a sky-blue sleeveless shirt trimmed in eyelet lace, with a matching yoked skirt. Casey told her how pretty she looked. Joanna thanked him. Joanna looked out the window and noted that the day promised to be a warm one. Casey agreed.

They went downstairs to another of Amanda's gourmet breakfasts.

After the dishes had been cleared away, Mike begged to be taken to Sand Pond.

He said, "Yesterday we saw that old museum, today can't we please have some fun?"

Sounding slightly hurt, Burnett said, "I thought you enjoyed visiting the museum."

Mike, a sensitive boy, immediately corrected himself. "I did, Uncle Burnett, really. But today I want to go to the Lakes."

Burnett argued that it might be too late in the year for good swimming, but Casey, who saw how much Mike wanted to go, told his brother he was taking Mike to Sand Pond. Period.

"Excellent," Mike said. "Can I ask Megan?"

"You bet," Casey told him. Then added, "Now, who else is coming along?"

Burnett gave in at that point and then everyone decided to go. Mike ran over to Megan's, but her family had other plans. He resigned himself to having fun without her.

Lillian and Joanna threw sandwiches together while Amanda complained that she'd had something so much nicer planned. They were ready to go before noon and took two vehicles: Casey's Blazer as well as the old Jeep that Lillian kept in the cabin's garage. Lillian rode with Burnett and Amanda in the Jeep.

As Casey drove the Blazer back over the Gold Lake Forest Highway, and Mike sang an endless song Megan had taught him about finding a peanut with innumerable improbable things inside it, Joanna felt her spirits lifting. Perhaps the key to putting up with in-laws wasn't in always going along with them, but in doing exactly what one wanted to do—cheerfully.

Before they reached Bassetts Station, they turned off the highway, crossed a bridge and took the lower of two roads past the Sardine Lake Campgrounds to a blacktopped parking area. Casey parked his truck in the shadow of a cedar tree and Burnett pulled the old Jeep into the space beside him.

Sand Pond was several hundred yards away, along any of a number of trails that wound through the trees. Everyone pitched in to carry the big cooler, the folding chairs, the rubber rafts and all the picnic gear along a winding trail to a favored site on the west side of the pond not far from the larger Lower Sardine Lake.

They chose a picnic table in a sunny spot among the trees and marshy grass. Burnett's prediction proved false; the water was still warm enough for swimming. The pond, which was never too deep even at its center, and as sandy as its name implied, lay low in the ground and was surrounded by trees, which protected it from the cold mountain winds.

Mike had barely set down the bag he was toting before he had his shorts and T-shirt off and was splashing around in the shallows near the shore. Lillian, too, stripped down to her swimsuit, but then sat in a folding chair in the sun, absorbed in her thriller.

"Ouch!" Amanda yelped. "These hideous big flies bite!"

"Heads up," Casey advised her, and tossed her the insect repellent. He then finished shucking everything but his swim trunks.

Joanna swam for a while, but then she remembered the glimpse she'd had of Lower Sardine Lake from the top of the rise between the lake and the pond. The glimpse had promised a beautiful view, one that cried out to be sketched.

She dried off quickly, slipped on her shoes and took the canvas tote that contained her sketchbook and pastels.

Lillian was engrossed in her book and Amanda sat by the picnic table, presumably guarding the lunch from the flies and the yellow jackets. Burnett was nowhere in sight; he'd probably gone for a walk.

Casey, Mike and a few children from the nearby campground were playing King of the Mountain. Joanna smiled to herself as she left them behind. Casey, like all good uncles, had the grace to be easily unseated when he was king and to experience great difficulty pushing sixty-pound children off the rubber raft when it was his turn.

The cold mountain wind whipped her hair wildly about her face when Joanna topped the rise. Joanna threw her head back and drew a big, glorious breath of it into her eager lungs. The lake, rimmed by huge chalk-white rocks and sat deep in a gorge of tall jewel-green pines, made her fingers itch with the need to start sketching.

She picked her way down among the sunbaked rocks, closer to the deep green surface of the lake, where the wind wasn't so fierce. But there, the sun was too bright, blinding her. So she moved toward Sardine Lake Lodge, on the northeast side, where the trees provided some sheltering cover. She sat beneath a fir tree, with a warm boulder at her back, and she began to draw.

For a while time had no meaning as Joanna lost herself in what she most loved doing. She'd filled several pages of her book with pastel strokes of color and images of the trees and the shimmering surface of the lake when she began to feel as if someone was watching her.

Slowly, she turned her head. Her brother-in-law stood not twenty feet away, outlined against the blinding brightness of the hot white rocks.

"Joanna," Burnett said, "I think it's time you and I had a little talk."

Chapter Fourteen

At first, Joanna didn't move. She looked at her brother-in-law without speaking, remembering all the promises she'd made to herself about this weekend—that her decision had been to avoid confrontations at all costs.

Then she thought that dodging showdowns just wasn't working. She and Casey were trying so hard to avoid family fights, that they'd ended up last night attacking each other, instead of their real targets.

There was too much hostility in the air. Throughout the weekend, they'd all been inhaling fuming resentment with every breath they took.

Maybe Burnett was right. It was time to confront a few things head-on.

Very deliberately, Joanna flipped the cover back over her sketchbook, then she put it and the pastels away in her tote bag.

"All right," she said. "We'll talk."

She had purposely chosen a sheltered spot, where the wind wouldn't tear at the pages of her sketchbook. The small, private indentation in the rocks was shaded by the fir overhead and a nearby pine: a beautiful spot. Joanna sighed. Too beautiful for what she suspected was going to occur between herself and Burnett.

She waited for Casey's brother to begin berating her. When he didn't, when he just stood there looking at her, Joanna began to feel impatient.

"Well, what is it?" she prompted.

He came closer, then, out of the blinding sun and beneath the haven of the trees. He sat down on a rock close to the one she was sitting on and he braced his forearms on his knees and folded his hands between them.

He looked at her intently. "What can I say to you, Joanna?" he asked, his voice low and controlled. "What can I do to make you see how wrong everything you're doing is? You're ripping this family apart."

Joanna's stomach tightened. It was unexpected, the tack he'd taken. Burnett sounded so *sincere*. His quiet intensity distressed her much more than his usual attitudes of hot rage or imperious command. It was clear that he firmly and passionately believed what he was saying. And the strength of his belief was convincing.

She had to consciously remind herself that there had been deeply rooted problems between Casey and Burnett even before she had ever met them.

"That's not true, Burnett," she said, careful to keep her tone calm and reasonable. "I am not and never have been the source of the problems in the Clinton family."

He was silent for a moment. Then he actually conceded her point. "Maybe not," he said. "But you *have* continually aggravated those problems, always making them worse when they might have improved."

"No, I—" Joanna started to protest, but Burnett didn't let her get the words out. He barreled on with his hurtful accusations, still in that low, troubled voice.

"You, Joanna, are a totally selfish person, only concerned with what you want at the moment, never thinking about the future, or about who might be hurt by the thoughtless things you do. You love yourself and yourself only, and you've been nothing but trouble for this family since the day we moved in next door to you all those years ago."

"Burnett, that's not true—"

Burnett clenched his fists. "Let me finish, please. For years, I've wanted to tell you what I think of you. You will do me the courtesy of listening now. Please."

Joanna drew in a long breath. "Burnett—"

"Please." It really wasn't a request, but for Burnett Clinton to utter that word—twice—was something Joanna had never expected to hear.

For a moment, she worried her lower lip between her teeth, thinking that listening to Burnett would do no one any good. But then, she thought that maybe it was only fair, maybe if he got it all off his chest, he would begin to let go of his anger toward her.

"All right, Burnett," she said at last. "But when you're done, you have to let me respond, to tell you what I think."

"Agreed," he nodded, a short chopping motion of his big head. For a moment, there was only the faraway laughter of the children in the pond over the rise, and the airy keening of the wind.

"Just like Casey, you are a person incapable of assuming adult responsibilities. And the two of you together are, and always have been, a disastrous combination. That's why I want you to admit that you've made another huge mistake in marrying my brother, and agree to return to Los Angeles where you belong."

Burnett paused, and for a moment Joanna hoped that he might actually be finished. It was a vain hope.

Burnett continued, "As I said at first, from the time you and Casey became friends, there has been nothing but trouble when you two got together. As children you egged each other on, from pulling fire alarms for fun to petty theft."

Joanna felt her face flushing. Once, when they were eleven, she and Casey had snitched a box of bubble gum from behind the counter at the corner store when the owner had turned away. They'd been caught an hour later when, having decided that robbery wasn't for them, they'd tried to return the box without getting caught. But guilt must have made them clumsy. When Joanna tried to slide the flimsy box back on the shelf, it had buckled in her hands, sending bubble gum raining all over the linoleum floor.

"We were kids," Joanna heard herself protesting. "Sometimes kids do things without thinking."

Burnett pinned her with a reproachful frown. "It's a habit you've never outgrown. As I was saying, you are bad for my brother. And you even played with *my* affections once upon a time."

Joanna drew in a breath. "Burnett, I was only eighteen when I said I'd marry you. My father had died. I was confused."

"Your mother told me you needed guidance," Burnett said. "And when I went to talk to you, you said you longed to be a different sort of girl than the one you were. I found myself asking you out—and you said yes. When I look back on it now, I remember that from our third date you were already hinting that you wanted to marry me."

"I was wrong," Joanna said.

"And then, out of the blue, you disappeared with my brother for two days and a night."

"I thought I could make my mother happy by marrying you," Joanna said. "It was all a mistake, that's all. People make mistakes, Burnett, no matter how hard you may find that to believe. We can't be dwelling on that for the rest of our lives. I regret any hurt I caused you, but it happened, and the best thing would be for both of us to let it go."

Burnett made a humphing sound, then he continued with his list of grievances. "You encouraged Casey to waste those years in the navy."

"It was what he wanted to do—and they were not wasted years."

Burnett went on as if he hadn't heard her. "I know you told him what a wonderful idea it was for him to throw his money away on that damned airfield."

"It was—and is—exactly what he wanted to spend his money on."

"Want, want, want. There is more to life, Joanna, than what you and my brother want." Burnett's face had grown flushed. He pounded a fist on his knee. Then he restrained himself again, with visible effort, and spoke more quietly.

"You've maintained a..." he sought the precise words, "...questionable long-distance liaison with my brother for years, always keeping your hooks in him just enough that he never found a suitable young woman to settle down with."

Joanna felt the blood rush to her cheeks. A liaison, indeed. It was too much. It was a totally absurd accusation.

Or was it?

The awareness of her newly discovered love washed over her. Could there be a grain of truth in what Burnett said? Had she been in love with her best friend for years—and simply not admitted it to herself?

When Casey's serious relationships had ended, he had always come to her. Never had she advised him to go back and try again. She had listened—as a friend should, she had thought—and made no judgments. There was nothing wrong in that.

Or was there?

Joanna found she could no longer just sit there while Burnett lambasted her. She stood up. "We're best friends, Casey and I. We always have been. Naturally we kept in touch over the years." Her voice had a high, defensive edge to it.

Burnett lifted his head to accuse piercingly, "You kept him dangling."

Joanna had to swallow before she could insist, "That's absurd."

"I'd say you always wanted to get him to marry you, for the sake of that ego of yours, though you knew my brother was no more likely to marry you than he was someone who might actually be good for him. You were just waiting for your chance."

"No. This is not true at all." Joanna put up her hands, as if the protective gesture could shield her from Burnett's farfetched assertions that somehow had the awful ring of truth.

Burnett continucd, relentless as an oncoming train. "You waited for your chance, and when it came you took it, becoming Mrs. Casey Clinton so that Casey would keep Mike, not even considering it was bad for Casey—and even worse for that poor little boy."

"That's a lie," Joanna uttered the words with conviction at last. However cloudy her own motives were beginning to seem to her, she remained absolutely certain that Casey was the one who should raise Mike. "It was the best thing for Mike. Casey is an excellent guardian. Emily made the right choice."

"And both you and my brother were willing to do anything, even marry each other, to see that Mike wasn't raised by me."

That was the brutal truth. Joanna opened her mouth to utter a resounding yes, when she caught the glint of triumph in Burnett's dark eyes.

He had set her up. This whole confrontation was a trap to get her to admit that her marriage to Casey was for one reason only.

Burnett stood. "Say it," he commanded. "Tell me the truth, Joanna. Admit your marriage is a fake, a put-up job to keep Amanda and me from giving little Mike the happy childhood he deserves."

Slowly, Joanna shook her head. "I love Casey," she said quietly. "And even if Mike wasn't involved, I'd marry him all over again. Maybe it's as you said, Burnett. I've always wanted to marry him, and I took my chance when it came."

Burnett's eyes grew stormy. "That's not what you were going to say a minute ago," he shot back. "You opened your mouth to say yes, to admit everything. I saw it, I saw it on your face." Joanna knew his anger was growing; he realized he had been thwarted.

"You saw wrong," she said, quiet and sure.

Something snapped in Burnett then, and he lost control. He reached out with punishing hands and took Joanna's shoulders.

"Damn you, Joanna!" he hissed through clenched teeth. "Admit the truth."

"I've told you the truth. Let go of me."

He gave her shoulders a shake. "By God I'll—"

He was stopped from saying what by Casey's voice. "Let her go, Big Brother."

Joanna and Burnett whipped their heads around. Casey stood on a huge boulder above them.

Burnett dropped his hands from Joanna's shoulders as if she'd burned him. "Go away, Casey. This is a private talk."

Casey jumped down from the boulder, landing beside them. "Whatever you want to call it, it's over."

Absurdly, Joanna found herself staring at the damp denim at Casey's hips, thinking that he must have pulled on his jeans over his wet swim trunks before coming to search for them. It was much easier to look at Casey's wet jeans than to witness the heated looks that arced between the brothers.

"Joey," Casey said. She was forced to look up into his ice-blue eyes. She knew he wasn't angry at her, but that didn't make seeing the rage in him any more bearable. He'd picked up the tote with her things in it, and was handing it to her. "Take this and go on back to the pond."

Here it was again. Just like fourteen years ago. They'd end up trading blows.

Joanna raised her chin. Damned if she was just going to walk away and let the two of them behave like adolescent boys.

"No," she said.

Both men glared at her.

"Leave, Joanna," Burnett said.

"Go on, Joey," Casey said.

"No."

Then Burnett made the error of reaching toward her, giving her a little shove to send her on her way. That was all it took for Casey. He punched his brother in the jaw.

Burnett, taken off guard, went down on his back among the rocks. He sat up. "Why you—"

He got no further, because there was a strangled sob from the rock where Casey had been standing a moment before. The three adults looked up.

Mike stood there. His face was a portrait of confusion and distress. Lillian, who appeared to have been following a small distance behind him, reached his side just as he cried, "Stop it! I hate it, everybody's always hurting everybody all the time!" Then he turned and ran, vanishing into the trees above the rocks.

"Mike, wait!" Lillian called, but the boy was already gone. Lillian turned back to the three below her.

"Joanna," Lillian said in a tone of absolute command. "Go after him. I'm not as fast as I used to be."

Joanna obeyed instantly, leaving Lillian standing, glaring down at her two miscreant sons.

Chapter Fifteen

Joanna caught up with Mike near Sand Pond. He'd stopped to slump against a tree trunk and rest for a moment, taking large, sobbing breaths into his small chest. Joanna's instinct was to run to him, gather his body against her own and hold him until he'd cried out all his hurt.

But she knew the reserved side of Mike's nature well enough to realize that coming on too strong might force him to withdraw.

She slowed to a casual walk and approached more circumspectly.

Mike saw her. "Leave me alone, Joey!" he shouted between sobs. "I don't want you!"

Joanna shrugged. "Okay," she said, and sat down on a quartz boulder that lay half-buried beside the path.

"I mean go away, Joey!" Mike hiccuped.

Just then, three children that Mike had been playing with earlier appeared on the trail. They were trying to roll a huge, ancient inner tube ahead of them and giggling as the tube wobbled and bounced down the path.

"Hey, Mike!" one of the kids called. "Come with us! We're rollin' this thing to the parking lot and back."

Mike swiped away his tears and waved, but shook his head. "Can't now."

The sight of him bravely smiling and greeting his new friends moved Joanna. Realizing that staring at him would draw attention to him when what he probably wanted most at that point was to be invisible, Joanna looked down at her feet. She studied the ground between her shoes, watching an ant climb the length of a fallen pine needle.

Soon enough, the children were gone. All was silent from the tree where, she hoped, Mike still stood. The ant Joanna was watching reached the end of the pine needle, crawled over her toe and then under the rock she was sitting on.

Joanna dared to look up. Mike was staring at her, still leaning against the tree. His lower lip quivered. Joanna stood up and held out her arms, and then knelt as Mike ran into them.

For a moment, she just held him, and then she took him away from the trail, deeper into the trees where they could talk alone. In a more private spot, they leaned against a pair of tree trunks, neither saying anything for a while.

Not surprisingly, the first person Mike spoke about when he was ready to talk was his mother. Mike said how much he missed her and how hard it was sometimes to think that she'd never be back.

"I do too, Mike," Joanna told him. "I miss her so much. I loved her a lot. And I just keep reminding myself that love is the one thing that never, ever dies."

"I loved her, too," Mike said, "so much. And if she could have not died it would have been good."

"Yes," Joanna said.

"But she did die," Mike said.

"Yes, Mike. She did."

"And now Uncle Burnett and Uncle Casey are always fighting. And Uncle Burnett pushed you. And Aunt Amanda is always mean to you. It isn't excellent, Joey. You know what I mean?"

"Yes, Mike. I do. I know exactly what you mean."

"It's all because I asked you never to go, isn't it?"

Joanna crouched down in front of Mike, putting her hands on his shoulders and waiting until he looked into her eyes. "No, it's not because of that," she told him. "It is honestly and truly not your fault at all. When you asked me to stay, then it was up to me to decide what I wanted to do. Staying was what *I* wanted to do. Do you understand?"

Mike looked back at her solemnly. "You mean, if things happened because you stayed, it's not my fault, it's your fault?"

Joanna sighed, wishing she were wiser. The rote answer would be that it was nobody's fault, but she felt too guilty to say that convincingly. "Let me put it this way: I stayed because *I* wanted to, so for you to blame yourself makes no sense at all."

"You mean it is your fault?"

In his child's relentless search for clarity, Mike was backing her into a corner. Joanna trotted out her rote answer after all. "Figuring out who's fault it is isn't going to solve anything, Mike."

Mike craned his head toward her and asked intensely, "But how can we make things better if we don't figure out what's wrong?"

Joanna could think of no immediate answer to that. She dropped her hands from Mike's shoulders and rocked back to a sitting position on the crunchy bed of dead pine needles that covered the ground. She decided to say what she felt. "I don't know, Mike."

Mike dropped to the ground and sat opposite Joanna, almost touching her, with his knees tucked against his chest, and his chin resting on them. His hazel eyes were piercing in their search for the truth. "Know what I really think?"

"What?"

"It's Uncle Burnett and Aunt Amanda's fault. I hate them."

Joanna had to look away. Hearing those ugly words from Mike was hard to take. Emily's dying wish was that her son, above all, be raised with love—and here he was talking of hate.

Joanna folded her legs Indian-fashion and found a pine needle to break apart, collecting herself before she spoke again. "That's sad, that you hate your Uncle Burnett and your Aunt Amanda," she said. "Because they love you very, very much."

Mike dismembered a pine needle of his own. "Okay, maybe I don't *hate* them."

Joanna said, "They sure do love you."

"Okay," Mike said. "Maybe I do love them, too."

He looked at Joanna, and she kept a neutral expression on her face. She was trying not to be judgmental. She'd decided to throw love in the face of hate and let the stronger win out.

"But they do bad things, and I don't like it," Mike added after a moment.

"Like what?"

"I told you already, Joey," he said, slightly miffed at her ostensible lack of attention.

"Tell me again, that way you can be sure I understand. Tell me the things they do that you don't like."

Mike said, very patiently, "Aunt Amanda does mean things to you. Uncle Burnett pushed you. And Uncle Burnett and Uncle Case are fighting all the time."

"Okay. Now what?"

He cast her an exasperated look. "That's all. Isn't that enough?"

"But what do you want to do about it?"

"I want them to stop."

"How would you make them stop?"

"Well, I could tell them." He thought for a moment, and then must have remembered what he'd said when he came upon the scene over the ridge at the lake. "Jeez," he added, "I guess I already did tell them."

Joanna smiled. "That's right. You sure did."

Mike said nothing for a moment as he broke another pine needle apart. Then he looked up. "I don't know what else to do, Joey."

"Well," Joanna shifted, curling her legs to the side and leaning on her hand. "Maybe you could wait and see if things change, now that you've told them."

"But what if they don't change?"

Joanna was grimly wondering exactly the same thing, but she didn't let Mike know it. She said, "*If* things don't change, *then* you worry about what you might do next. For right now, you've done all a six-year-old boy possibly could."

"I have?" He looked doubtful, but very eager.

"Absolutely. Besides that, you've realized that it is not your fault if Amanda and I don't get along, or if your uncles fight—right?"

"Right." He nodded, a quick, decisive gesture. Then he leaned back against the tree trunk and squinted up through the thick cover of pine branches over their heads, as if pondering what he'd just learned.

Joanna wondered if there was more she ought to say. It occurred to her then that raising children was a truly humbling experience. You were just never smart enough or wise enough or half as loving as you knew you ought to be.

"Joey?" Mike asked, when a few moments had passed with only the blue jays and the squirrels saying anything.

"Um?"

"I think we ought to go back now, don't you?"

"Yes," Joanna said. "I think that would be a good idea." They stood up and returned to the trail together.

* * *

When they reached the picnic spot by the pond, the others were all there. Amanda, the only one of the group who hadn't been involved decided it was her place to take things in hand.

"Well, it's about time we all got here," she announced as Mike and Joanna appeared. "It's getting late. It's after two o'clock. And no one's eaten lunch." Keeping up a steady stream of chatter, she urged them all to sit around the redwood table. Then she served up the sandwiches Joanna and Lillian had made.

For Mike's sake, Joanna assumed, everyone tried to make lunch as pleasant as possible. Casey and Burnett behaved toward each other with civility; Burnett even attempted one of his rare ponderous jokes. Amanda filled every silence with overly bright comments about nothing in particular. Joanna did her best to keep her end of the conversation going. And Mike was subdued but cheerful.

Of them all, Lillian was the silent one. As they drove back to Graeagle in the late afternoon, Joanna realized that Lillian had barely spoken two words since she'd curtly commanded her to go after the fleeing Mike.

It was the same over dinner. Lillian sat, barely touching her food, her gaze focused on each of the faces around the table in turn. It was as if she was studying each one of them, Joanna thought, as if she was evaluating them all through new eyes.

"Mother, that look!" Amanda complained at one point. "It's positively penetrating. Do I have spinach between my teeth?"

"No, not at all," Lillian said. It was the largest number of words she'd strung together all afternoon.

Amanda tittered, and then apparently decided the subject was better left alone.

After dinner, Mike paid his evening visit on Megan, and Casey asked Joanna to walk with him down by the Mill Pond. Joanna tugged on a sweater and went with him, her heart heavy with a sense of foreboding.

They strolled side by side, but not touching. The dragging sadness around her heart seemed to increase. Joanna knew that she only had to reach out to clasp Casey's hand, but somehow his manner discouraged such a gesture.

Casey seemed far away from her again. It was hard to remember that only the day before yesterday this same man had playfully tackled her to the sweet grass behind the cabin and wrestled with her there, finally kissing her into giggling submission.

When they stood by the water with the sun low in the sky behind them, Casey asked what had happened when she'd caught up with Mike. Joanna told him.

"You're good with him, Joey," he said when she was finished.

"You would have done as well—or better," she maintained.

He chuckled then, but without much humor. "Even a couple of confirmed bachelors can learn how to be parents, I guess—given the proper motivation and the necessary circumstances."

Joanna forced herself to chuckle, too. "I guess so."

They strolled on, past clumps of willow bushes to a place where they could stand right at the water's edge. Joanna thought of Lillian.

"What happened," she asked carefully, "after Lillian sent me to find Mike?"

Casey knelt, picked up a smooth, round stone and tossed it overhand out into the pond. When it dropped beneath the surface, the concentric ripples flowed toward the shore. Casey spoke just as the ripples, faint from traveling so far, reached their feet.

"Mother ordered Burnett to tell her what had happened." Casey's voice was flat, as if he wanted to give the information without injecting any of his feelings on the events. "Burnett explained what happened more or less honestly, at least from the point where I came on the scene."

"He didn't say what had happened between him and me?" Joanna asked.

"He said you were having a *little talk.*"

"Oh."

Still in a crouch, Casey tossed another stone. "Then Mother asked him what your talk was about."

"And?"

Casey looked up at her. His light eyes were shadowed, his mouth a grim line. "Burnett said that that was between you and him."

Joanna said, "He was trying to get me to admit that I only married you so that he wouldn't get Mike."

"I figured that," Casey said.

Joanna longed to tell Casey everything that had passed between herself and Burnett. But that would hit too close to the tender subject of her newfound love, and this was a bad time to get into that.

Furthermore, Burnett's cruel accusations had put a new and harsh light on her own actions. She needed time to think about the hard things Burnett had said, to face them or to reject them before confessing them to Casey.

Casey continued, "I know my big brother. He thinks he's protecting Mother, by not telling her what he and Amanda have been up to since you and I got married."

"But, earlier, he told her he was going to sue you for custody," Joanna said.

Casey explained patiently, "That was before we married, when he at least had his two-parent argument to make him sound somewhat reasonable. If he told her now that he's still after custody, he'd have to upset her by saying he thinks our marriage is phony. And who knows how she'd react to that.

"No, he thinks it's better to get us to break up first, and then tactfully let her know that he's taking Mike away from me—for Mike's sake, of course."

Joanna couldn't restrain a disgusted groan. "Does he think that Lillian's an idiot? She knows as well as anyone else does what's going on."

Casey's voice was flat. "Burnett knows exactly what he's doing. Mother plays ostrich about the problems between him and me; Burnett's just making it easy for her. He's careful never to give her any direct information that she might feel she has to actually do something about."

Joanna shook her head in frustration at the whole situation. Then she told Casey, "I didn't admit anything to Burnett."

"I never thought you did." Casey threw several stones in succession, so that the tiny ripples as their feet came at a faster rate.

"What happened next?" Joanna asked.

Casey stood up. "Nothing." Joanna looked at him, perplexed. He went on. "Nobody said anything for what seemed about a century. Then Mother said 'all right, let's go back.' And she left. Burnett and I stood there for a minute, feeling like a couple of prize jerks—or at least, *I* felt like a jerk—then I picked up your bag with your sketchbook in it and went back to Sand Pond. He followed after me."

Out on the Mill Pond the fish had begun to feed. Joanna caught a glimpse of a shimmering white belly, surging up, twisting, and then flopping back beneath the smooth water. Soon the swallows would come.

"Casey," she said. "We just can't keep on like this. It's terrible for Mike—and for all of us, really."

"I know," Casey said. "I think it's come to a parting of the ways."

Joanna swallowed; she thought for a moment that he was telling her their marriage was over.

But then he continued, "I'm through with these family events. I'm through pretending I can get along with my brother and his wife. It's been nothing but disaster every time we've tried. I brought you out here to say I want to leave tonight, and to tell you that seeing either Burnett or Amanda again is off unless things somehow really change."

"But Casey..." Despite everything, Joanna hated to see the break happening. The love between Burnett and Casey was steeped in conflict, but they *were* brothers. "Cutting them out of our lives isn't any kind of solution."

"Maybe not, but right now it's the only thing we can do, I'm afraid. Mike's had enough pain in his six years on this earth. Damned if I'll see him suffer any more than he has to." He took a deep breath, then added with a sad quirking of one eyebrow. "Maybe someday..."

"Yes," Joanna nodded, forcing a smile. "Maybe someday."

The first swallows soared above when they turned away from the pond and strolled back toward the cabin, side by side, but not touching.

Lillian was waiting for them on the porch. "I've done some thinking. And I'd like to talk to everyone. Right now. Burnett and Amanda are waiting in the kitchen."

Casey said, "There's no point, Mother. Let it be. We're going home."

"That's up to you," Lillian told him. "But there's something I'd like to say to all of you first."

Casey drew a long breath. "I'm tired of it, Mother. I'm fed up to here. Can't you understand that?"

"Completely," Lillian said.

"Good. Is Mike still at Megan's?"

Lillian nodded. "He came back and asked if he could stay overnight. I said I thought it would be all right, so he took his pajamas over there. But I know he'll understand if you've decided to leave. He's an incredibly reasonable child."

"All right," Casey said. "Joey, you start getting things together and I'll go get Mike."

Rather than do as he'd said, she murmured his name.

"What is it?" He glanced at her absently, eager to collect his nephew and be on his way. "What?" A frown creased his forehead. Then, reading her expression, he knew what she wanted.

He said, "No, Joey. Just let it be."

Lillian left them alone, silently passing back into the house.

Joanna said, "Casey, let your mother have her say."

"Nothing anybody says ever makes things any different."

"Yes, but Lillian's never spoken up before. She has a right to speak, and it's our place to listen."

He shook his head, his eyes showing a bottomless weariness. "I want to go."

"I understand," Joanna said. "And I know that I should stop pushing you."

Casey smiled then, a smile that would have made her lose her heart to him, if it hadn't already been entirely his. "But you're not going to stop pushing me, is that it?" he said.

She nodded, smiling in return. "That's it. I'm hoping you won't make me beg."

He looked at her, a deep look that made her stomach flutter. "Would you beg me, Joey?"

"Absolutely. In this situation."

"I owe you. A hell of a lot," he said.

She didn't want him to owe her. She wanted him to love her. But this wasn't the time to talk about that. She wondered, miserably, if the time would ever come.

"Does that mean we'll hear Lillian out, then?" she finally asked.

"Only because you asked me," he said.

"Fine. Whatever it takes."

She went up the steps. He followed reluctantly, but he did follow, nonetheless.

They all took chairs at the big rectangular pine table in the kitchen, each of them armed with a cup of coffee and a wary, vigilant expression.

Burnett sat at the head of the table, but it was Lillian who held firm control.

She began by saying that she had always tried her best to stay out of the conflicts between her sons. Not until this afternoon, had she seen the extent of her error—at least when it came to the question of Mike.

"It is time," Lillian announced, "that I made it clear where I stand."

Joanna looked around the table. Burnett was doing his best to look unruffled, though the tightness around his eyes gave his anxiety away. He seemed a little too quiet, actually, Joanna thought. Then she realized that he was feeling badly about what Mike had witnessed that afternoon.

In spite of his overbearing nature, Burnett was not evil. However misguided his methods, he loved his family and wanted the best for them. To have been caught behaving so shamefully by the boy he sought to protect was probably weighing on his conscience.

Amanda, sitting to Burnett's left and across from Joanna, displayed her nervousness with every move she made. She kept taking tiny sips from her coffee, setting the cup down, and then immediately picking it back up again. Lillian sat next to her, her handsome face set in determined lines. Casey, opposite Burnett, had turned his chair and leaned his chin on the back-rest. He looked comfortable and relaxed, as he always did—revealing nothing of the turmoil Joanna knew must be going on inside him.

Joanna herself rested her arms on the table, her cup between them. Her coffee was untouched.

Lillian continued, "What Mike was forced to witness this afternoon must never be allowed to happen again. We all—" she paused, to glance piercingly at each of them in turn "—are *adults.* That means it is our responsibility to behave as such in the presence of children."

Amanda set down her cup with a little clink and complained, "I still don't quite understand what exactly happened. I stayed behind to guard our lunch, and—"

Burnett said flatly, "Joanna and I had words, Amanda. Casey interrupted us. We asked Joanna to leave and when she wouldn't, I pushed her. Then Casey punched me. Mike saw that and ran."

"Why, that's terrible," Amanda said. She aimed a withering look across the table at Joanna and then asked her husband, "What kind of words did you and Joey have?"

Lillian cut in, her voice icy. "You may ask him that later, Amanda. As far as this meeting goes, that's a side issue."

"Well," Amanda said. "Pardon me." She grabbed her cup again and gulped down another sip.

"The main issue," Lillian went on, "is that somehow Mike's guardianship seems to still be in dispute."

Burnett made a sharp sound in his throat, and Amanda's cup hit the table again.

"I can't see why you're so surprised that I'm aware of what's going on in my own family, Burnett," Lillian pointed out. "You did, after all, tell me you planned to take Casey to court for custody before he married Joanna. And I'm not blind, you know. It's been obvious that you and Amanda have done everything short of breaking the law to drive a wedge between Casey and Joanna since the day they exchanged vows."

"That's unfair and uncalled for, Mother," Burnett said in his most impressively imperial tone.

"Is it?" Lillian challenged.

"Yes."

For a long moment, Lillian just stared at her oldest son. And then Burnett seemed to come to a decision.

He said, "All right. Do you want to get it all out in the open, Mother? Is that what you're asking for?"

"This is precisely what I want." Joanna thought that Lillian had never sounded so resolute.

"Fine, then," Burnett said. "Let's deal first with that so-called *marriage* that Casey and Joanna are involved in."

Casey said, "No, let's not." Although his voice was low, soft as velvet, it brought a moment of charged silence in its wake. He went on. "My marriage to Joanna is *our* business and our business alone."

Burnett stood up and and accused blankly, "Not if it's a farce—a fake you engineered to keep the boy away from me."

The two men glared at each other, down the length of the table.

Then Casey stood up, too. "There's no point in continuing this," he said. "Joanna, we're leaving."

Lillian reached out. She put her hand on Casey's arm. "Please, just let me finish." She turned to Burnett. "Will you please sit down."

Slowly, both brothers dropped back into their seats.

Then Lillian spoke again. "Casey is absolutely right. His marriage with Joanna is none of your business, Burnett." Burnett drew an outraged breath. "I'm not finished," Lillian said, before Burnett could speak. "It was Emily's wish that Casey raise Mike. And I thoroughly agreed with her."

Amanda gasped, a wounded sound.

"You what?" Burnett's voice was hollow, shocked.

"I agreed with her," Lillian repeated, slowly drilling each word home. "You are a good man," she said, facing Burnett squarely. "And you have been the backbone of this family since Edward left us. But you lack essential qualities that Mike needs—patience, tolerance, a sense of humor. I am sure that you could have learned to develop these qualities, were you the only choice as guardian. But you were not the only choice. There was also Casey, and he possesses these qualities already. Moreover, since he returned home from overseas, he has found himself work that fulfills him and is happy here at home. So along with the other qualities I've mentioned, he is stable and satisfied with his life. He is absolutely the superior choice to raise Mike, and I never intended to allow it to be otherwise."

Amanda, whose lovely face had grown crimson, could no longer contain herself. "But what about me?

Didn't you even consider me? *I'm* a better choice as a mother than—"

Lillian cut her off with a look. "I know you want a child, Amanda," she said. "And someday, I'm sure you will have one. But Mike is not that child. Accept it."

Amanda withdrew with a small, stricken sob. Very slowly, Lillian let her gaze sweep the table, making sure she had everyone's undivided attention. The gesture was a formality only. She held them all riveted.

"Single or married," Lillian said at last, placing a slow, meaningful stress on each of the words, *"Casey will raise Mike.* And I will stand behind him one-hundred percent." Once more she turned a penetrating look on Burnett. "If you take Casey to court, you'll be taking me, too. By the time you have finished, you will have driven away both of us, and you will have done damage to an innocent child."

Burnett sat very still gazing back at his mother. And then his big shoulders seemed to visibly slump.

Joanna glanced at Lillian, and caught the look of sympathetic anguish that flashed briefly in the older woman's eyes. This was her own son Lillian was being forced to hurt, and it caused her great agony to do so.

Burnett seemed unable to speak, and no one else could bear to.

Then Lillian spoke, keeping her voice low and even. "Have I made myself clear at last?"

Burnett coughed into his fist, and forced his shoulders to straighten. He said, with great and quiet dignity, "Yes, perfectly clear."

Lillian sat very straight in her chair. She folded her hands on the table. "Does that mean there will be no more harassment of Casey and Joanna? And no more talk of lawsuits?"

Burnett said, "Yes. It's over. I can't fight you both."

Amanda, who had been gripping her coffee cup in a stranglehold, suddenly burst into tears and stood up, knocking her chair over with a loud crash. "That boy needs a home!" she cried between sobs. "A real home! I could give him that, but instead, you're going to let her raise him!" She cast Joanna a quick, vicious look and fled from the room, trailing sobs.

Burnett quietly rose. "Forgive her," he said. "You have no idea how badly she wants a child." He went up the stairs after his wife.

When Burnett was gone, the silence lay over the bright kitchen like a pall. Joanna sat looking at her cold coffee, wishing that what had just been accomplished could have been done in a gentler, less hurtful way.

Lillian's words, when she spoke, echoed Joanna's thoughts. "I didn't want to have to do it," she said. Outside, the shadows thickened as night approached. "I hated to do it. And it doesn't really make things any better, does it?"

"It makes them clearer," Casey said. "And it's the right thing for Mike. That's what counts."

Lillian patted his hand. "You're right, of course." Then she asked him again to stay the night.

Casey looked at Joanna, who nodded. Then he said they would.

It was full dark when Burnett came down the stairs alone. Amanda, he explained, was already in bed. They wanted to get an early start for home tomorrow.

Then he asked Casey to go for a walk with him. Casey agreed.

When the two men were gone, Joanna and Lillian found themselves looking at each other across the knotty surface of the old table.

Lillian smiled. "Come out to the back porch with me."

Joanna stood up, and carried her cold coffee to the sink. "I don't know, Lillian. I was thinking of going up to bed."

"Please?"

The word was said to Joanna's back, and she thought of Burnett that afternoon, saying *please* before he told her all the ugly things he'd been storing up for years. Lillian, of course, had really meant the word. It was a request, not a command.

And Joanna never could say no to a request from Lillian. She turned, and gave Lillian a smile in return. "All right."

Outside, they sat together under the kitchen window, on the wooden couch with the cracked canvas cushion. The trees that rimmed the yard looked ghostly in the moonlight, like the shadows of mythical night creatures crouching just beyond the circle of silvered grass.

"The stars are so much brighter up here," Lillian said.

Joanna gave a small noise of agreement, and rested her head against the window frame. She closed her eyes.

Lillian's next question took her totally by surprise, "Joey, do you love my son?"

Perhaps the dramatic events of the day had made her numb. She heard herself asking, "Which son, what kind of love?"

Lillian chuckled. "Casey. Are you in love with Casey?"

Without turning her head to her mother-in-law, or opening her eyes she said, "Yes."

"But you weren't in love with him when you married him?"

It didn't even occur to Joanna to obscure the truth. And keeping the true nature of their marriage a secret was no longer necessary, not after tonight anyway.

"No," she said. And then she thought of Burnett's accusations that had hurt too much not to have some truth to them. "Or if I was in love with him then," she amended, "I didn't know it."

"Have you told him how you feel?"

"No."

"When are you going to tell him?"

"I don't know. Soon."

The two women were silent for a while. "I'm so happy, Joey," Lillian said.

Joanna suddenly wanted to cry. "Why?"

"Because I think you two have been in love forever, but you just haven't realized it."

"Lillian, I don't think Casey's in love with me," Joanna said, this time turning to seek out the older woman's eyes in the darkness.

"Oh, certainly he is. Of course he is. Emily and I have always known it."

Hope, like something so hot it burned, flared in Joanna's heart. "Did Casey tell you that?"

"Well," Lillian looked away. "No, he never said it in so many words, but—"

Joanna didn't want to hear anymore. "Don't," she said. "Let's drop it, and please don't say anything to Casey."

"Of course not. That's for you to tell him." Lillian leaned a little closer. "You *will* tell him, though?"

Joanna rubbed her eyes. "Let it go, Lillian. Please."

Lillian sank back to her side of the couch. "I'm sorry. I've done so much interfering today, it's becoming a habit, I'm afraid."

"You were brave and wonderful," Joanna said.

Lillian grunted. "I kept putting off the confrontation, hoping I could save us all the pain. As a result, I ended up causing everybody more pain than was necessary."

"It's settled now," Joanna said.

"That's what happens when you don't do what needs to be done," Lillian elaborated somewhat archly. "Things only get worse."

Joanna took Lillian's meaning and turned it in her mind. It was true, she knew. That was why, right now, it hurt to hear it said.

"Oh Lillian," Joanna said very low. "Since we got married, I've lost my best friend."

Joanna felt the soft, dry touch of Lillian's hand on hers. "Tell him," Lillian said.

Lillian was right, Joanna admitted to herself. They couldn't continue like this: talking but not talking—together but miles apart. Joanna needed to get the truth out in the open right away.

But not tonight, she hedged silently. Not upstairs in that room with Burnett and Amanda on the other side of the wall from us. I need absolute privacy to tell him how I feel...

But then she realized that there would always be one excuse or another to keep her from revealing the secret of her heart. Tonight, it would be lack of privacy. Tomorrow, that she had to get ready for the flight to Los Angeles. And then, all this week would be taken up with preparing for the show. And then she'd need to focus on the bank commission...

Joanna almost chuckled aloud. If she planned it right, she could keep from telling Casey she loved him until both of them were old and gray—or at least, she thought wryly, remembering her words to Casey the night before—until Mike was in college.

"When will you tell him?" Lillian prodded gently from the other end of the couch.

"Tonight," Joanna answered. "I'll tell him tonight, as soon as we're alone."

Chapter Sixteen

When Joanna and Casey were alone in their upstairs room, Joanna asked first about how things had gone between Casey and his brother. Casey told her that he and Burnett had walked to the Graeagle Meadows Golf Course and back. Nothing of significance had been said.

"But it was better between you, wasn't it?" Joanna asked. She wanted to hear that it was. She wanted to hear some good news before she told Casey she was in love with him. That way, if her confession brought on rejection, she could console herself with the knowledge that something good had still come of all this: two brothers had made the first hesitant steps toward healing the wounds of a lifetime.

Casey, however, refused to be too optimistic. He said, "Joey, it's going to take a lot more than an evening stroll to fix what's wrong between Burnett and me."

"But it's the first step."

"I suppose."

"That's wonderful."

Joanna thought of Amanda, with whom she would probably never make real peace. The thought made her sad. But, then, if she and Casey split up, it probably didn't matter at all how she got along with Amanda Clinton. Her relationship to Burnett's wife would be terminated—no marriage, no sister-in-law.

That thought made her sadder still, so she ordered her mind to stop dwelling on the negative.

Joanna had perched on the edge of the bed when she entered the room. Casey was standing near the door. Both of them were still fully clothed. The space between them seemed to vibrate with uneasiness—as if all of the things unsaid bounced and swirled in the air, invisible, but nonetheless profoundly disturbing.

"Well," Casey said, leaving the other side of the room and walking to the bow window, which was behind her. Joanna had to turn around to look at him as he finished, "I guess we should get ready for bed."

"Right," Joanna said, standing up. She felt a coward's sense of temporary relief. She would get ready for bed—and *then* she'd tell him she loved him.

Taking comfort in having something to do, she pulled the T-shirt she was wearing over her head, tossed her bra on the bed and shimmied out of her jeans. She took her nightgown off of the peg behind the door and stuck her arms through the sleeves, gathering the material, before she stuck her head through the collar. She glanced up at Casey watching her.

Reflexively, she smiled, and pulled the wad of nightgown against her bare breasts.

"Think I'll go downstairs for a cup of hot chocolate," he said.

Joanna blinked. "But, Casey, I—"

He came toward her quickly, and was around her and out the door before she could say any more.

"You go ahead and turn off the light," he said just before he shut the door between them. "I'll be a while."

Joanna dropped the nightgown over her head and went back to the bed. She slumped down upon it.

I should follow him downstairs, she thought glumly. But her nerve was gone.

Alone, she crawled between the covers of the bed.

The next morning, Burnett and Amanda left before Mike returned from Megan's. Amanda wore dark glasses and said little as they carried their luggage out to their car. Once the suitcases were stowed in the trunk, she got in on the passenger side and waited for her husband to be ready to leave.

It was Burnett who surprised Joanna. He hugged his mother and his brother. They were rather formal, stiff hugs—but they were hugs nonetheless.

Most amazingly, before he climbed in behind the wheel he looked up to where Joanna stood a few feet away.

He said, "Joey, we'll see you at home."

Joanna knew that that was as close to a request for a truce as she'd ever get from Burnett Clinton.

She nodded. "Yes, see you soon, Burnett," she said.

Burnett got in his car and backed out of the wide gravel driveway.

Mike returned soon after that, and Casey and Joanna were ready to go. Lillian stayed on for a few hours. The caretaker was due to stop by and Lillian needed to give him a few added instructions.

Casey took them home by the route along the Feather River and through Quincy. They reached Sacramento before noon. They unpacked, ate lunch and swam. Then one of Mike's friends, who lived across the street, called and asked him over for hotdogs. Mike was given permission, but told to return by seven sharp.

Joanna went upstairs and began packing again for the trip to Los Angeles the next day. As she packed, she rehearsed her declaration of love.

She would make that declaration tonight, she'd decided, if she had to tie Casey to the bed to get him to listen to her.

Most of her clothes were still in the studio room, so she was riffling through the closet in there when Casey came to talk to her.

He sat on the end of her supply table. "I've been thinking about L.A.," he said.

Joanna hooked a blouse she'd been considering back onto the closet rod and glanced over her shoulder at him. Her heart seemed to have lifted and paused in her chest. She waited for it to start pounding again, before she said, studiously casual, "Oh? What about it?"

"Well, maybe you'd rather go on down by yourself," he said.

Joanna just looked at him. The phrases she'd been rehearsing played in her mind:

Casey, it has become clear to me over the past few weeks that I love you in a much deeper, more profound sense than I had previously realized...

Casey, I feel more for you than I've told you...

Casey, I not only love you, I'm in love with you...

"It *is* Mike's first day of school tomorrow," Casey was saying.

The plan had been that Casey would go with Joanna, and that Lillian could come stay with Mike. Then Casey would fly back to collect Mike on Friday afternoon so Mike could be there for the party at the gallery that opened Joanna's one-woman show.

The two of them at last spending some time without their ready-made family had been an intimate joke between them; they'd finally be able to explore all the erotic possibilities of her apartment.

"I kind of feel I should be here for Mike's first day of school," Casey continued. Then he laughed, an utterly false laugh. "What good am I going to be to you anyway down there, right? You'll be busy getting things set up with Althea, and all that."

Of course, that was true. Setting up a gallery for an art show could be a hectic, demanding process. Everybody from the program printer to the caterer always considered himself an artist in his own right. It could end up being three days of tempers and temperaments. Maybe that was the last thing Casey wanted right now. Perhaps he needed a little more time to himself after the mess at Graeagle. Joanna could understand that, however much it might hurt.

Joanna reached for the blouse that she'd already decided not to take, and concluded that she needed it after all. She carried it over and slid it into the garment bag that lay on the daybed.

The litany of her unspoken declarations kept playing in her mind.

I love you, maybe I always have...

And not only as friends...

But as a woman loves a man...

Casey was fiddling with some of her brushes that were standing handles down in a coffee can. "And I've been thinking that maybe we could both use the space."

Space. At the mention of that word, something snapped inside Joanna. She whirled on Casey.

"Space," she said, planting her hands on her hips. "That's what you think we need? More *space?*"

Casey looked stunned. "Yeah," he said rather dumbly. "What's wrong with space?"

"Space," she repeated, injecting all her frustration into the single word.

His expression wasn't so confident now. "That's what we need—isn't it?"

"Is it?"

He looked as befuddled as a game show contestant who just can't seem to find the correct answer to the sixty-four thousand dollar question. "It isn't?"

"Not as far as I'm concerned," she said. "As far as I'm concerned, all we've got is space. We've got so much space, we don't talk to each other, so much space, we don't touch each other. And you think we need *more* of it?''

''Joey,'' he said, still nonplussed at the sudden change in her. ''Settle down . . .''

''Space,'' she said the words again, as if it left a disgusting taste in her mouth, ''is the last damn thing we need.''

''Joey, I thought you wanted—''

''You thought I wanted?'' She stopped, halfway across the room, spun on her heel and faced him directly. ''How could you possibly have the slightest idea what I wanted, Casey Clinton? For weeks now, you've been either making love to me or leaving the room the minute it looks like I might actually *say* anything!''

They stared at each other. Finally, Casey stood up. ''All right,'' he said grimly. ''Tell me. Go ahead and tell me.''

She narrowed her eyes at him. ''You won't suddenly decide you have log sheets to take care of?'' she said, wary now—and frightened. The moment was upon her. Lord help her, she didn't want to blow it.

''I'm not moving from this spot,'' he told her.

''All right,'' she said.

''Fine,'' he said.

They stared at each other.

Then she said, ''Casey, I—''

And he said, ''Joey, listen—''

Both fell silent.

After endless seconds, they said simultaneously, ''What?''

They looked at each other again.

Joanna began to feel foolish poised in the middle of the floor. She went to the daybed, pushed the garment bag aside and sat down. Then she slipped off the sandals and drew her legs up under the hem of the drop-waisted sundress she wore.

Oddly, she was conscious, even within her apprehension, of a new feeling of relief. At least it was going to all be said. By the time they left this room, they would know where things stood.

Across from her, Casey had stood up. He looked confused and uncomfortable, totally at a loss for what to do or say next.

Joanna said, "It's not easy anymore, is it?"

"What?" He sounded defiant, even angry.

"Talking to each other. We've gotten so out of practice."

"There are things," he said, still defiant, "that I just have trouble talking about. It's all too new. It confuses the hell out of me."

"What things?"

He looked away. "I thought you wanted to say something."

"But so do you, am I right?"

He looked back at her. "Yes."

"Go ahead," she told him. "You go first."

He went to the bay window over the side yard. He looked out. Then he seemed to force himself to face her again, to say what he was going to say while looking into her eyes.

"All right," he said. "Something really strange has happened, something I never thought would happen to me. Something I'm not very comfortable with, something that's hard for me to talk about."

"My Lord, what?" she asked, aching for him, because he looked so absolutely miserable.

"I love you, Joey," he said. "And I don't mean only as a friend. But as a man loves a woman."

Chapter Seventeen

Joanna stared at Casey. "Could you say that again?" she finally asked.

"I'm in love with you. Maybe I always have been, I don't know about that for sure."

Her heart had stopped—this time with joy. "Oh, I see," she heard herself murmur idiotically.

"When Emily was dying..."

"Yes?"

"She told me I was in love with you," Casey said. "She said that we should be together, and that together we could make a home for Mike. I humored her, saying I'd do what I could about that."

In Joanna's mind, Lillian's words echoed. *Of course he's in love with you. Emily and I have always known it...*

Casey went on, "You know how Emily was, so frail, almost . . . transparent at the end. You could see the blood in her veins through her skin."

"I remember," Joanna said.

Casey went on, "I would have agreed to just about anything she asked for then, and not thought twice about it."

"I can understand that."

"But the strange thing was, after she was gone, I couldn't quit thinking about it, about what she'd said. That I was in love with you. And when you insisted on coming here to help out, and I was around you every day, I thought about it more and more." He sat down on the window seat, and stuck his hands in the pockets of his slacks. He looked down at his feet, then back up at Joanna. "But I kept telling myself it wasn't true. I'd always thought of myself as someone who didn't want any forever kind of commitments. I accepted myself that way. And then, to start having these . . ." he had to search for the words, " . . . forever kind of thoughts, about you, well, I pushed them from my mind.

"And it worked," he went on, "for those first few weeks you were here. We had had so many years of practice in relating to each other in a certain way. I could keep it friendly and affectionate, and my own dangerous thoughts never came up." He looked at her narrowly. "You never guessed, did you? At first, when you came here to stay?"

"No," she told him honestly. "I didn't have a clue."

He laughed, a dry sound. "But then, Burnett decided to take me to court, and I heard myself announcing that we were getting married—and it hit me.

Marrying you was *exactly* what I wanted. Because Emily was right. I am in love with you."

Joanna said, "You mean you've known for sure since the night you announced we were getting married?"

He nodded. "I came to your room that night to tell you, to get it all out in the open. But you were so beautiful, and I thought..." he paused, then he pulled his thoughts together. "I thought that if I scared you away by telling you too soon, I'd blow my chances for making you love me back."

Joanna tipped her head to him, knowing he wasn't telling the whole truth, but having no idea what he was leaving out.

"All right," he said, reading her expression as he always could. "Maybe right then it was a little more basic than that. I wanted to make love to you. What I really thought that night was that we'd never make love if I spilled everything too soon and scared you off.

"So I took advantage of the situation with Mike to get you to marry me," Casey's voice was steeped in self-disgust. "I thought I could make you love me, eventually. I didn't realize what should have been obvious."

"And that is?"

"That starting the whole thing on a lie would eat at me. That it would get harder and harder to tell you how I felt." He shook his head, his expression one of sad wonder. "My own idiocy amazes me. I wanted you so badly, so I tried not to rush you."

"By not making love to me on our wedding night, you mean?"

"Right. And then later, when we finally made love in L.A., and you told me you'd been ready all along, I could see that you must have felt I didn't want you then. But somehow, I couldn't tell you the truth about that without telling you *everything*. By then I'd convinced myself that if I told you everything, it would only make things worse. So I started making love to you whenever it looked as though we might be getting too close to the truth. I believed I was *showing* you how I felt, rather than actually saying it. But it was really just another excuse for not taking the risk of losing you altogether.

"And then," he said grimly, "there was Burnett and Amanda. Naturally, they made you their prime target. It became like some never-ending nightmare. I wanted to make you love me—and what I did was push you away and set you up to be victimized by my family."

"Nobody victimized me," Joanna said. "I chose to marry you and I accepted the consequences."

Casey waved his hand in front of his face, indicating that he didn't buy her interpretation. "Whatever."

"There's no *whatever* about it, Casey. That's how it was—and is. I'm willing to accept responsibility for my own actions. Believe it. Mike does, and he's only six."

He stood up. "Anyway, I thought after this weekend you'd want to get as far away as possible from me and the rest of the Clintons. So that's why I suggested you could have your week in L.A. alone."

"I see."

"And," he continued. "We have to face the fact that what Mother did this weekend changes everything."

"It does?"

He glared at her. "It's obvious that it does. You don't have to stay married to me any more. Mike stays with me, whether we're married or not."

"Yes," Joanna smiled at him. "It's wonderful, isn't it?"

"You do want your freedom, then?" Casey asked, his voice flat.

"Are you asking me or telling me?"

He looked angry again. "Isn't that what this is all about?"

"No."

"What do you mean, no?"

"No, it isn't about freedom, if by that you mean another word for space. I don't want space, I want my best friend back. And I want to keep the marriage we've made together."

"Damn it, Joey," he said. "Don't be kind to me. I think I could take just about anything right now, but you being kind."

Joanna stood up. "Don't worry, I'm not."

"Not what?"

"Being kind."

"Then what?"

Slowly, she approached him. "I'm trying to find a way to tell you."

"What?"

"What I've been longing to tell you." She felt like her bare feet weren't even touching the floor. She felt she floated toward him.

"So do it. Tell me," he said.

She stopped before him. "I love you."

"You *what?*"

"I love you. And as much more than a friend. As a woman loves a man."

"But—"

"Yes?"

"How long have you known that?"

"At least since last Friday, when Burnett and Amanda caught us kissing on the back lawn. But maybe longer. Maybe years. Burnett thinks I've always been lying in wait for you..." She paused for a moment, just to breathe in his nearness. Slowly, she took the collar of his sport shirt and pulled him even closer than he already was. "...Like a spider in her web," she said in a sinister tone.

Casey's lips were so close, she could have reached out and kissed them. And she intended to, very soon.

He said, "Burnett said that?"

She nodded. "Yesterday. He said I had kept you from ever finding a suitable woman to marry. And you know what?"

"I'm listening." He was watching her lips with extreme concentration.

"He might be right," she confessed. "I never wanted you to marry anyone else, not really. I think, deep down, I was always a little jealous of the other women you cared for. But we both had so many things we wanted to do in life. It took a little boy who needed us to be together to make us see what the other people we loved knew all along."

"And that is?"

"Didn't I just say it?"

"I wouldn't mind at all if you say it again. It's not the kind of thing a man gets tired of hearing from the woman he loves."

"Okay, I'll say it again. We were meant to be together. I'm in love with you, and now that I've got you, Casey Clinton, I'm never letting you go. Understand?"

He was quiet. He gave her one quick, tempting kiss. "Well, I don't know," he said.

"What?"

"Maybe you should explain more thoroughly..."

"Maybe you should tell me you're going to L.A. with me, like my best friend would."

"All right. I'm going to L.A. with you."

"Good. And maybe we should also agree that, from now on, whatever happens, no matter how hard it is to talk about—we *will* talk about it, like best friends should."

"Agreed," he told her, kissing her once more, pulling her close to his heart, so that something inside her kindled and then flamed.

His lips moved over hers, tender and seeking—then hungry and demanding. And Joanna responded in kind.

And once he had kissed her so thoroughly that her whole body had turned to molten desire in his arms, he kissed her some more, waltzing her across the room as he did it, until he could close and lock the door to the landing.

At that point Joanna opened her eyes and asked drowsily, "Why, Casey Clinton, what is going on?"

His answer came against her lips as he began kissing her again. "We're about to explore the erotic possibilities of this very room—starting with that drawing board over there."

She pushed at his chest. "What? You're nuts." She eyed the drawing board. "Uh-uh, no way. Not on that..."

"Joey..." he was kissing her ear. "Let's just try it."

"No way," she said firmly.

But then he said, "I dare you..."

She pulled back to meet his eyes.

He looked at her; she looked at him.

"You dare me?" she asked.

"I double dare you," he said then.

Joanna laughed, a woman's laugh, full of knowing and promise and just a touch of coyness. Then she opened her arms to him—her best friend, her lover, and the companion of her heart.

* * * * *

by

LINDSAY McKENNA

Dawn of Valor

In the summer of '89, Silhouette Special Edition premiered three novels celebrating America's men and women in uniform: LOVE AND GLORY, by bestselling author Lindsay McKenna. Featured were the proud Trayherns, a military family as bold and patriotic as the American flag—three siblings valiantly battling the threat of dishonor, determined to triumph . . . in love and glory.

Now, discover the roots of the Trayhern brand of courage, as parents Chase and Rachel relive their earliest heartstopping experiences of survival and indomitable love, in

Dawn of Valor, **Silhouette Special Edition #649.**

This February, experience the thrill of LOVE AND GLORY—from the very beginning!

DV-1

Silhouette Books